THE ADVENTURES OF PROFESSOR THINTWHISTLE AND HIS INCREDIBLE AETHER FLYER

By DICK LUPOFF and STEVE STILES

WILDSIDE PRESS

WILDSIDE PRESS

ISBN: 978-1-4344-1004-7
Published by Wildside Press LLC
www.wildsidebooks.com

Cover design by Stephen H. Segal.

INTRODUCTION

My Dear Lupoff,

Your letter, having been conveyed across the wide Atlantic by packet steamer, arrived today at a most salutary moment. Indeed, I was breaking my fast this morning and pondering the wondrous miracles that progress brings us, year in, year out; the sun shone brightly on my eggs and toast, and outside the window the merry voices of the street people were raised in raucous joy as they twitted each other with the catch-phrases of the day: "Twopence more, and up goes the donkey!" they called, one to another, and "Has your mother sold her mangle? Ho, call again tomorrow, Vicar, and we'll have a crusty one!"; and it was at that moment that the housemaid brought me your missive, and the packet of illustrated text you enclosed with it.

Is it not a remarkable world we live in, in which you may write a letter in California, and a mere matter of months later, it arrives at my door, here in the British Isles?

To answer your question — and indeed, to put you out of the miseries you must now be going through even as you read this — the answer is yes: I would indeed be delighted to pen a brief introductory note for your remarkable tale of Professor Thintwhistle, and his Aether flyer. Indeed, should you so wish, you might consider publishing this very letter, as a preamble to your fine work.

As to what I think about Thintwhistle? Sir, I think three things, which I shall list here.

Firstly, the tale is scientifically educational and of much worth. I rejoice to think how many young minds (both young men and, if I may presume, perhaps even some bluestockings) may be awoken to the delights of scientific advancement by such a palatable introduction to the concepts of the properties of the Aether, of Phlogiston, even of the rarefied mysteries of Gravitational Attraction, through your tale.

Secondly, it is inspiring: who can but thrill at the achievements of the Learned Professor, of Clarence, his noble protege, as they make their way into the sky? What heart of stone could gaze up into the summer night having read this, and remain unmoved by the possibility that one day a human foot — clad, I presume, in the sturdy leather footwear of a Briton or American — will make its imprint upon the surface of the fair Luna?

Thirdly, is it morally instructing. The youth of today, alas, tends toward the cheap and meretricious delights of the Penny Dreadful, morally void and sensational works which debase and degrade the reader. If but one impressionable child is drawn away from the lure of Varney the Vampire, or Her Guilty Secret, then, my dear Lupoff, you will have done humanity a great service. Incidentally, I must say I find your technique of combining words with pictures one that has great merit, and one that may, indeed, as you Americans so quaintly say, "catch on." I have taken the liberty of suggesting to Mr Dickens that he write to the estimable Mr Stiles to discuss the possibility of their collaborating in this nascent medium. Do you have a name for this unique mode of graphic literature?

On the evidence of Thintwhistle, I do not feel it is overstating matters to suggest, my dear Lupoff, that you may well be the equal — nay, the superior — of our young English writer Mr. Wells, or of Verne, the Frenchman, in your imaginings: I feel you are the pinnacle of a new triumvirate.

I have showed your tale to my good friend (and member of the Royal Society) Professor D_____, and I must tell you that he questioned the scientific plausibility of the Aether Flyer: he maintains that a vehicle of the nature you posit here would need far more coal than you illustrate to make a voyage to a destination as far away as the Moon, and that your Professor would need to take an entire Welsh mining village with him, were he to travel to the stars. But, you will be pleased to learn, he opines that the Thintwhistle Aether Flyer would be far more practical than firing a craft to the sky from the barrel of a gun, as Verne himself suggested.

D_____ was also dismayed by the pictorial representation of Selena, the Queen of the Moon; but as I explained to him — forcefully, as you may tell from my language, "Dash it all, D_____, it is no more than one can see hanging in the Tate Gallery, or carved from the finest marble in the vast halls of the British Museum," and he was forced to agree. But his is a scientific mind, and not an artistic one. Mr Stiles and yourself handle these matters with tact and discretion, and should Mrs Grundy cavil, we can but say, "Humbug, Ma'am!" and leave her to her Philistinism.

I trust that you are in good health. Please reassure Messrs Groth and Thompson, your publishers, that I desire no honorarium for penning these pensees; after all, it is enough to know that I am, in my own small way, helping to keep the flame of progress burning, as we head inexorably towrad the bright and splendid dawn of the Twentieth Century — and towards wonders that, I suspect, not even your Professor Thintwhistle could imagine.

Let us all dream of a world in which Mankind may harness the power that hides itself in the heart of a nugget of common housecoal, and travel to the most distant stars!

Yours as ever,
NEIL GAIMAN

THE ADVENTURES OF PROFESSOR THINTWHISTLE AND HIS INCREDIBLE AETHER FLYER

WRITTEN BY DICK LUPOFF

ILLUSTRATED BY STEVE STILES

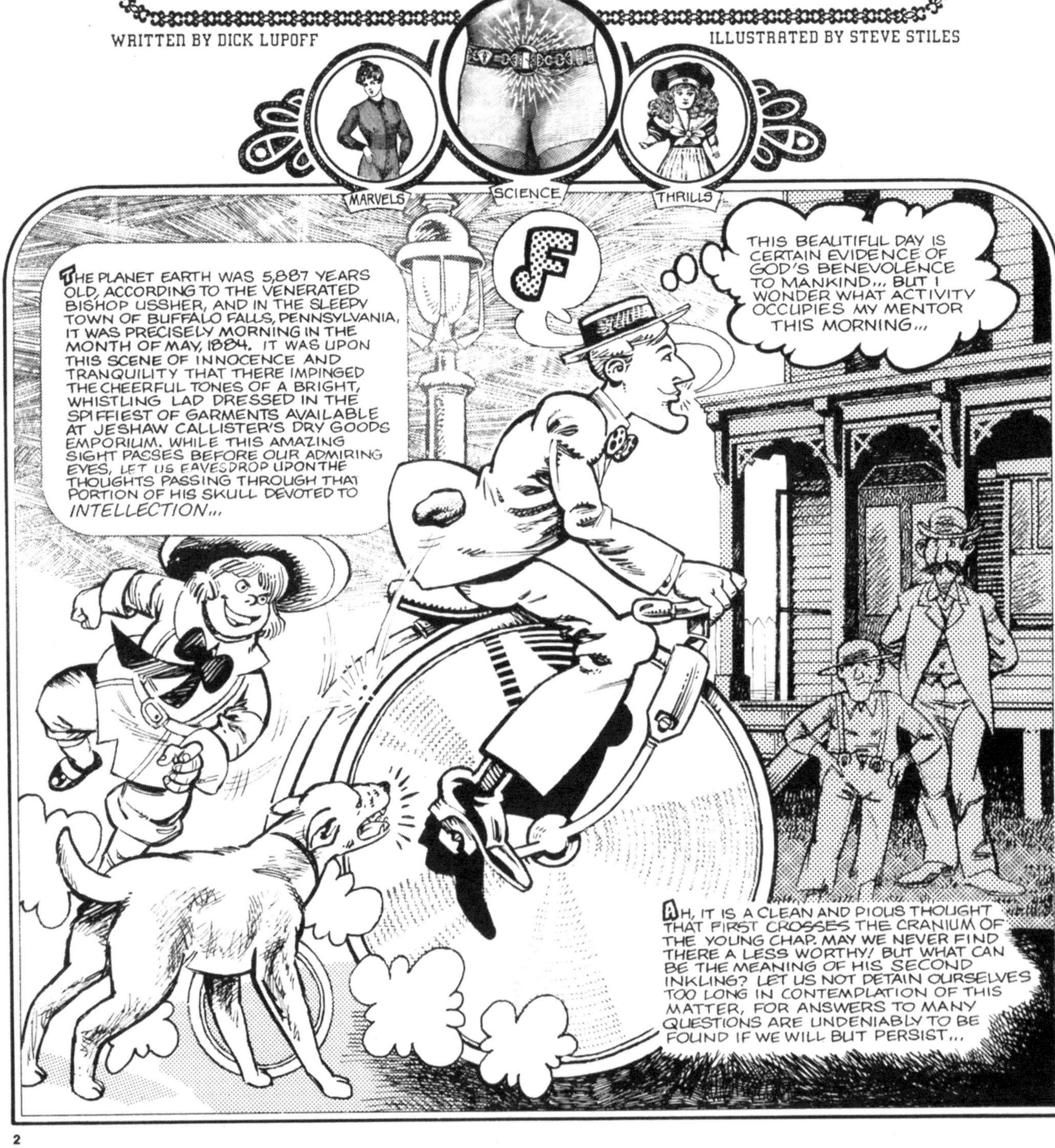
MARVELS
SCIENCE
THRILLS
THE PLANET EARTH WAS 5,887 YEARS OLD, ACCORDING TO THE VENERATED BISHOP USSHER, AND IN THE SLEEPY TOWN OF BUFFALO FALLS, PENNSYLVANIA, IT WAS PRECISELY MORNING IN THE MONTH OF MAY, 1884. IT WAS UPON THIS SCENE OF INNOCENCE AND TRANQUILITY THAT THERE IMPINGED THE CHEERFUL TONES OF A BRIGHT, WHISTLING LAD DRESSED IN THE SPIFFIEST OF GARMENTS AVAILABLE AT JESHAW CALLISTER'S DRY GOODS EMPORIUM. WHILE THIS AMAZING SIGHT PASSES BEFORE OUR ADMIRING EYES, LET US EAVESDROP UPON THE THOUGHTS PASSING THROUGH THAT PORTION OF HIS SKULL DEVOTED TO *INTELLECTION*...
F
THIS BEAUTIFUL DAY IS CERTAIN EVIDENCE OF GOD'S BENEVOLENCE TO MANKIND... BUT I WONDER WHAT ACTIVITY OCCUPIES MY MENTOR THIS MORNING...
AH, IT IS A CLEAN AND PIOUS THOUGHT THAT FIRST CROSSES THE CRANIUM OF THE YOUNG CHAP. MAY WE NEVER FIND THERE A LESS WORTHY! BUT WHAT CAN BE THE MEANING OF HIS SECOND INKLING? LET US NOT DETAIN OURSELVES TOO LONG IN CONTEMPLATION OF THIS MATTER, FOR ANSWERS TO MANY QUESTIONS ARE UNDENIABLY TO BE FOUND IF WE WILL BUT PERSIST...

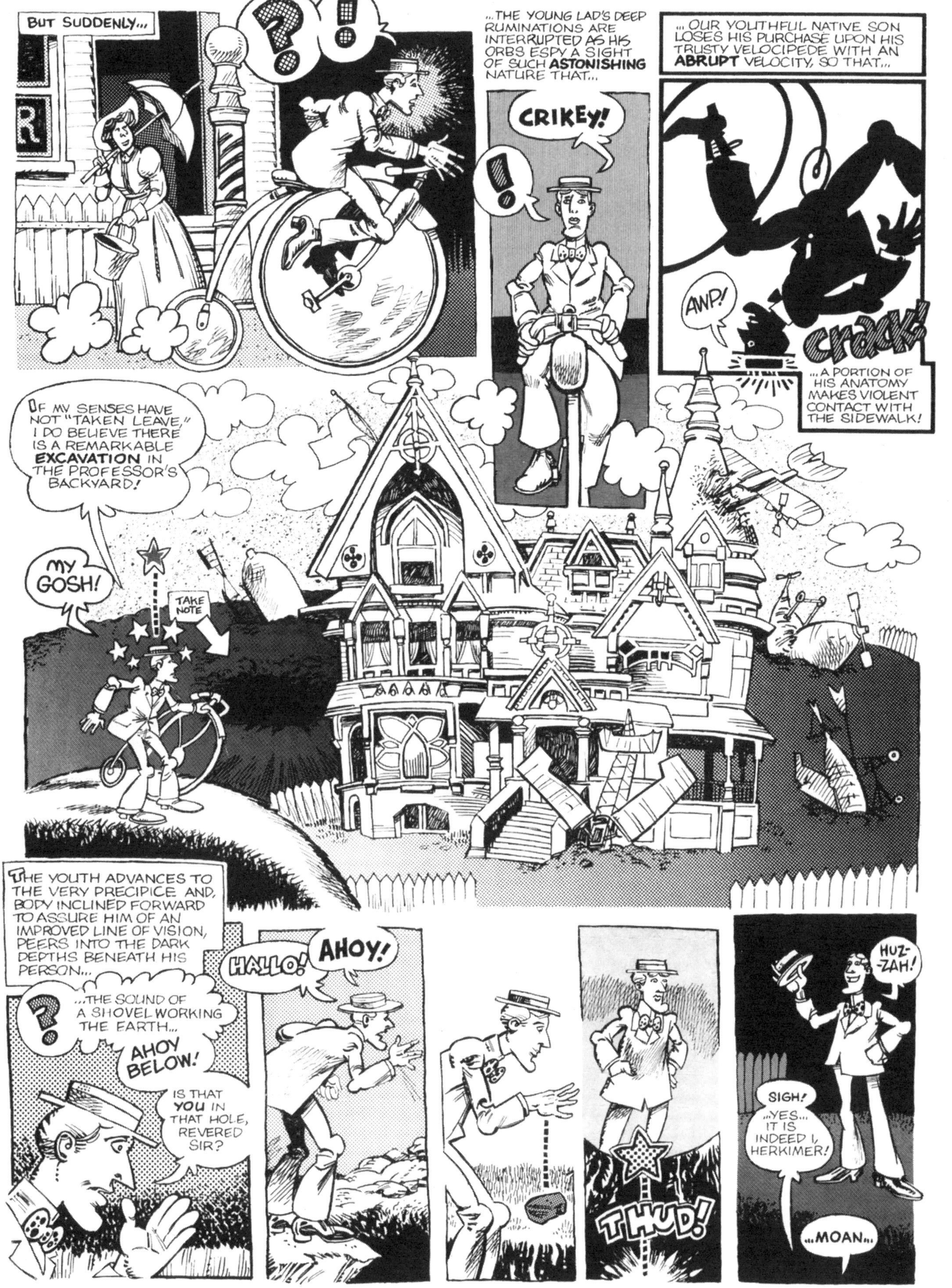

BUT SUDDENLY...
?!
...THE YOUNG LAD'S DEEP RUMINATIONS ARE INTERRUPTED AS HIS ORBS ESPY A SIGHT OF SUCH ASTONISHING NATURE THAT...
CRIKEY!
!
...OUR YOUTHFUL NATIVE SON LOSES HIS PURCHASE UPON HIS TRUSTY VELOCIPEDE WITH AN ABRUPT VELOCITY, SO THAT...
AWP!
CRACK!
...A PORTION OF HIS ANATOMY MAKES VIOLENT CONTACT WITH THE SIDEWALK!
IF MY SENSES HAVE NOT "TAKEN LEAVE," I DO BELIEVE THERE IS A REMARKABLE EXCAVATION IN THE PROFESSOR'S BACKYARD!
MY GOSH!
TAKE NOTE
THE YOUTH ADVANCES TO THE VERY PRECIPICE AND, BODY INCLINED FORWARD TO ASSURE HIM OF AN IMPROVED LINE OF VISION, PEERS INTO THE DARK DEPTHS BENEATH HIS PERSON...
?
...THE SOUND OF A SHOVEL WORKING THE EARTH...
AHOY BELOW!
IS THAT YOU IN THAT HOLE, REVERED SIR?
HALLO!
AHOY!
THUD!
HUZ-ZAH!
SIGH!
...YES... IT IS INDEED I, HERKIMER!
...MOAN...

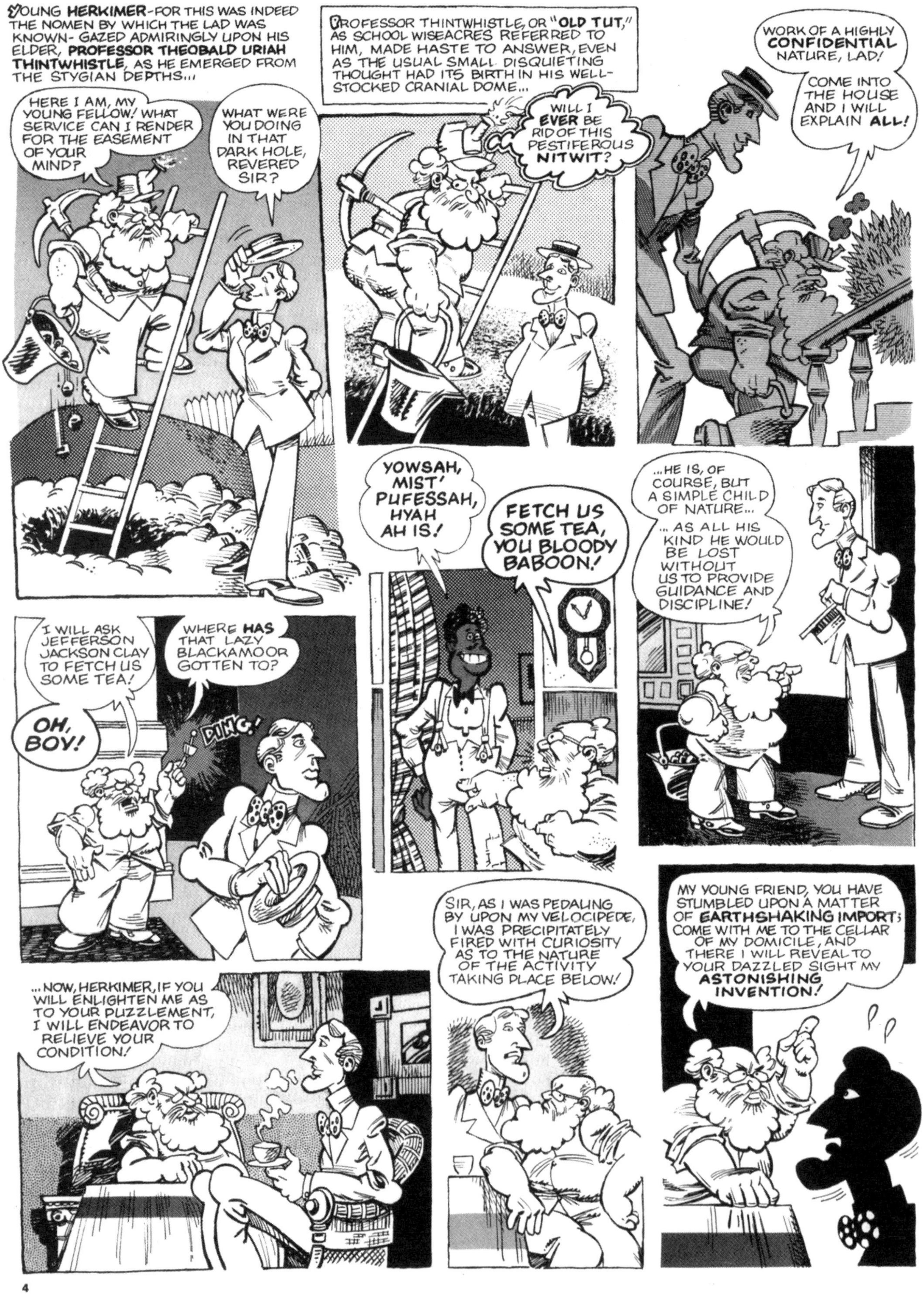

YOUNG HERKIMER-FOR THIS WAS INDEED THE NOMEN BY WHICH THE LAD WAS KNOWN- GAZED ADMIRINGLY UPON HIS ELDER, PROFESSOR THEOBALD URIAH THINTWHISTLE, AS HE EMERGED FROM THE STYGIAN DEPTHS...
HERE I AM, MY YOUNG FELLOW! WHAT SERVICE CAN I RENDER FOR THE EASEMENT OF YOUR MIND?
WHAT WERE YOU DOING IN THAT DARK HOLE, REVERED SIR?
PROFESSOR THINTWHISTLE, OR "OLD TUT," AS SCHOOL WISEACRES REFERRED TO HIM, MADE HASTE TO ANSWER, EVEN AS THE USUAL SMALL DISQUIETING THOUGHT HAD ITS BIRTH IN HIS WELL-STOCKED CRANIAL DOME...
WILL I EVER BE RID OF THIS PESTIFEROUS NITWIT?
WORK OF A HIGHLY CONFIDENTIAL NATURE, LAD!
COME INTO THE HOUSE AND I WILL EXPLAIN ALL!
I WILL ASK JEFFERSON JACKSON CLAY TO FETCH US SOME TEA!
OH, BOY!
WHERE HAS THAT LAZY BLACKAMOOR GOTTEN TO?
DING!
YOWSAH, MIST' PUFESSAH, HYAH AH IS!
FETCH US SOME TEA, YOU BLOODY BABOON!
...HE IS, OF COURSE, BUT A SIMPLE CHILD OF NATURE...
...AS ALL HIS KIND HE WOULD BE LOST WITHOUT US TO PROVIDE GUIDANCE AND DISCIPLINE!
...NOW, HERKIMER, IF YOU WILL ENLIGHTEN ME AS TO YOUR PUZZLEMENT, I WILL ENDEAVOR TO RELIEVE YOUR CONDITION!
SIR, AS I WAS PEDALING BY UPON MY VELOCIPEDE, I WAS PRECIPITATELY FIRED WITH CURIOSITY AS TO THE NATURE OF THE ACTIVITY TAKING PLACE BELOW!
MY YOUNG FRIEND, YOU HAVE STUMBLED UPON A MATTER OF EARTHSHAKING IMPORT; COME WITH ME TO THE CELLAR OF MY DOMICILE, AND THERE I WILL REVEAL TO YOUR DAZZLED SIGHT MY ASTONISHING INVENTION!

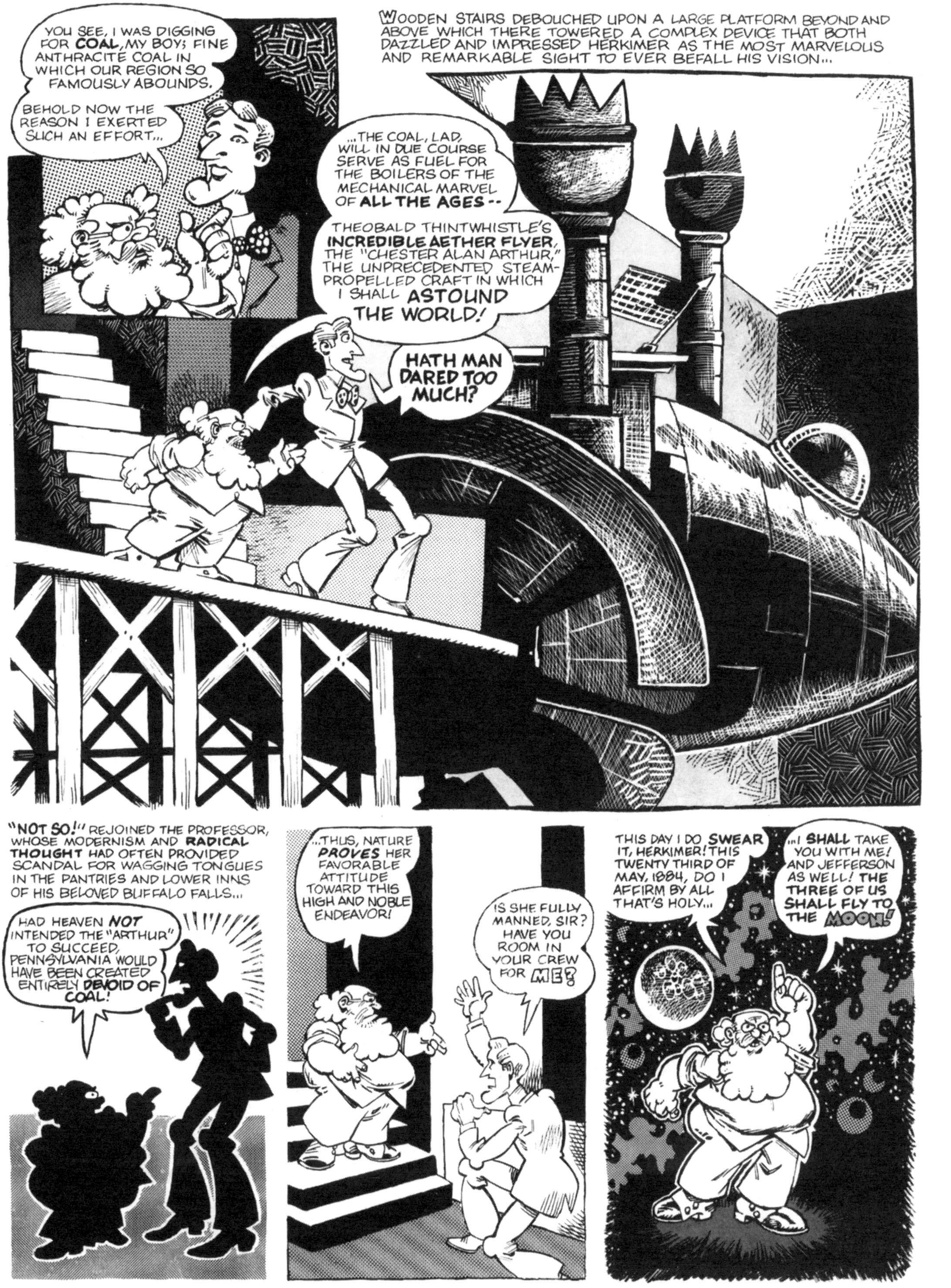
YOU SEE, I WAS DIGGING FOR COAL, MY BOY; FINE ANTHRACITE COAL IN WHICH OUR REGION SO FAMOUSLY ABOUNDS.
BEHOLD NOW THE REASON I EXERTED SUCH AN EFFORT...
WOODEN STAIRS DEBOUCHED UPON A LARGE PLATFORM BEYOND AND ABOVE WHICH THERE TOWERED A COMPLEX DEVICE THAT BOTH DAZZLED AND IMPRESSED HERKIMER AS THE MOST MARVELOUS AND REMARKABLE SIGHT TO EVER BEFALL HIS VISION...
...THE COAL, LAD, WILL IN DUE COURSE SERVE AS FUEL FOR THE BOILERS OF THE MECHANICAL MARVEL OF ALL THE AGES --
THEOBALD THINTWHISTLE'S INCREDIBLE AETHER FLYER, THE "CHESTER ALAN ARTHUR," THE UNPRECEDENTED STEAM-PROPELLED CRAFT IN WHICH I SHALL ASTOUND THE WORLD!
HATH MAN DARED TOO MUCH?
"NOT SO!" REJOINED THE PROFESSOR, WHOSE MODERNISM AND RADICAL THOUGHT HAD OFTEN PROVIDED SCANDAL FOR WAGGING TONGUES IN THE PANTRIES AND LOWER INNS OF HIS BELOVED BUFFALO FALLS...
HAD HEAVEN NOT INTENDED THE "ARTHUR" TO SUCCEED, PENNSYLVANIA WOULD HAVE BEEN CREATED ENTIRELY DEVOID OF COAL!
...THUS, NATURE PROVES HER FAVORABLE ATTITUDE TOWARD THIS HIGH AND NOBLE ENDEAVOR!
IS SHE FULLY MANNED, SIR? HAVE YOU ROOM IN YOUR CREW FOR ME?
THIS DAY I DO SWEAR IT, HERKIMER! THIS TWENTY THIRD OF MAY, 1884, DO I AFFIRM BY ALL THAT'S HOLY...
...I SHALL TAKE YOU WITH ME! AND JEFFERSON AS WELL! THE THREE OF US SHALL FLY TO THE MOON!

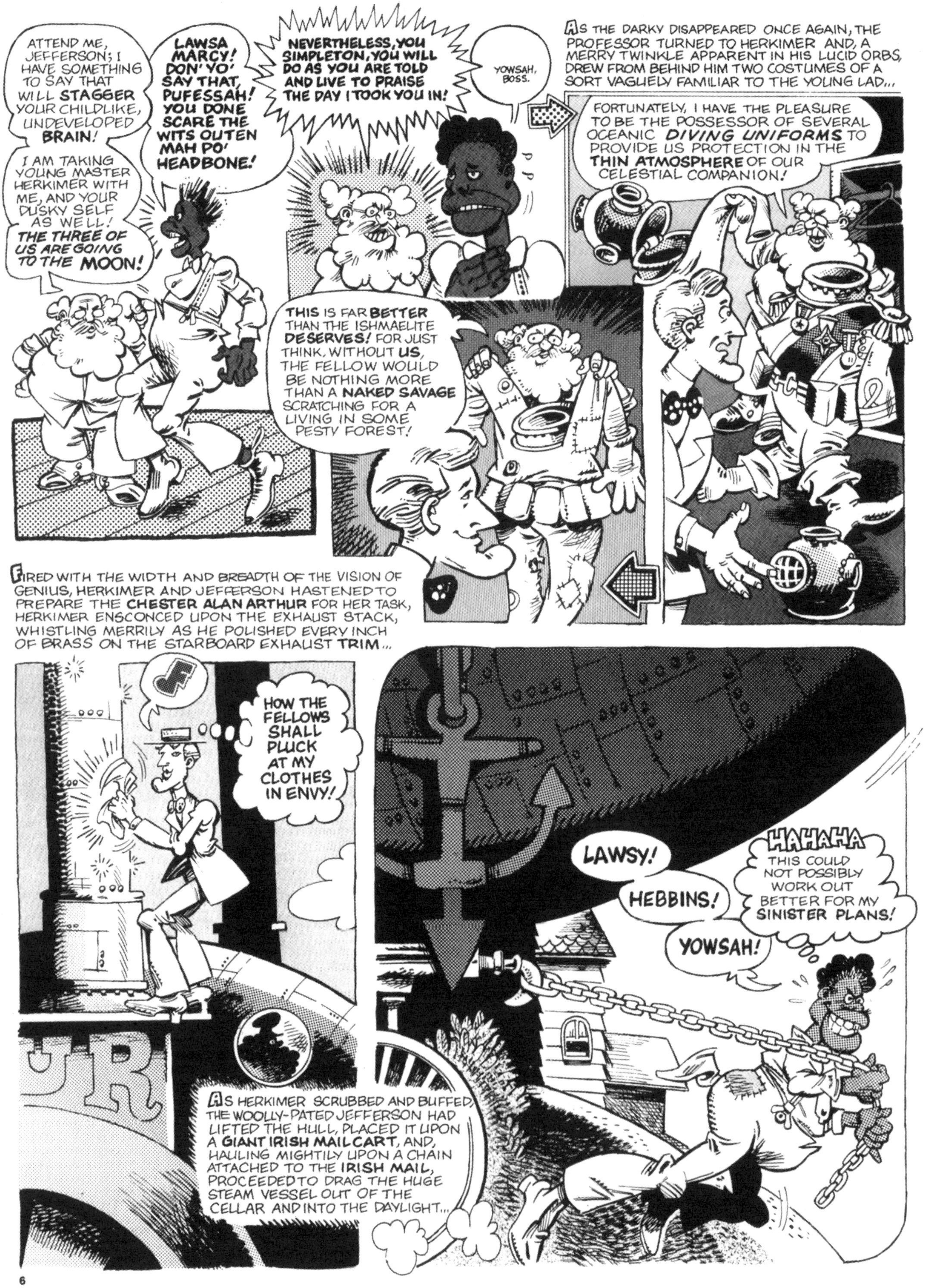

ATTEND ME, JEFFERSON; I HAVE SOMETHING TO SAY THAT WILL STAGGER YOUR CHILDLIKE, UNDEVELOPED BRAIN!
LAWSA MARCY! DON' YO' SAY THAT, PUFESSAH! YOU DONE SCARE THE WITS OUTEN MAH PO' HEADBONE!
I AM TAKING YOUNG MASTER HERKIMER WITH ME, AND YOUR DUSKY SELF AS WELL! THE THREE OF US ARE GOING TO THE MOON!
NEVERTHELESS, YOU SIMPLETON, YOU WILL DO AS YOU ARE TOLD AND LIVE TO PRAISE THE DAY I TOOK YOU IN!
YOWSAH, BOSS.
THIS IS FAR BETTER THAN THE ISHMAELITE DESERVES! FOR JUST THINK, WITHOUT US, THE FELLOW WOULD BE NOTHING MORE THAN A NAKED SAVAGE SCRATCHING FOR A LIVING IN SOME PESTY FOREST!
AS THE DARKY DISAPPEARED ONCE AGAIN, THE PROFESSOR TURNED TO HERKIMER AND, A MERRY TWINKLE APPARENT IN HIS LUCID ORBS, DREW FROM BEHIND HIM TWO COSTUMES OF A SORT VAGUELY FAMILIAR TO THE YOUNG LAD...
FORTUNATELY, I HAVE THE PLEASURE TO BE THE POSSESSOR OF SEVERAL OCEANIC DIVING UNIFORMS TO PROVIDE US PROTECTION IN THE THIN ATMOSPHERE OF OUR CELESTIAL COMPANION!
FIRED WITH THE WIDTH AND BREADTH OF THE VISION OF GENIUS, HERKIMER AND JEFFERSON HASTENED TO PREPARE THE CHESTER ALAN ARTHUR FOR HER TASK, HERKIMER ENSCONCED UPON THE EXHAUST STACK, WHISTLING MERRILY AS HE POLISHED EVERY INCH OF BRASS ON THE STARBOARD EXHAUST TRIM...
HOW THE FELLOWS SHALL PLUCK AT MY CLOTHES IN ENVY!
UR
LAWSY!
HEBBINS!
YOWSAH!
HAHAHA THIS COULD NOT POSSIBLY WORK OUT BETTER FOR MY SINISTER PLANS!
AS HERKIMER SCRUBBED AND BUFFED, THE WOOLLY-PATED JEFFERSON HAD LIFTED THE HULL, PLACED IT UPON A GIANT IRISH MAIL CART, AND, HAULING MIGHTILY UPON A CHAIN ATTACHED TO THE IRISH MAIL, PROCEEDED TO DRAG THE HUGE STEAM VESSEL OUT OF THE CELLAR AND INTO THE DAYLIGHT...

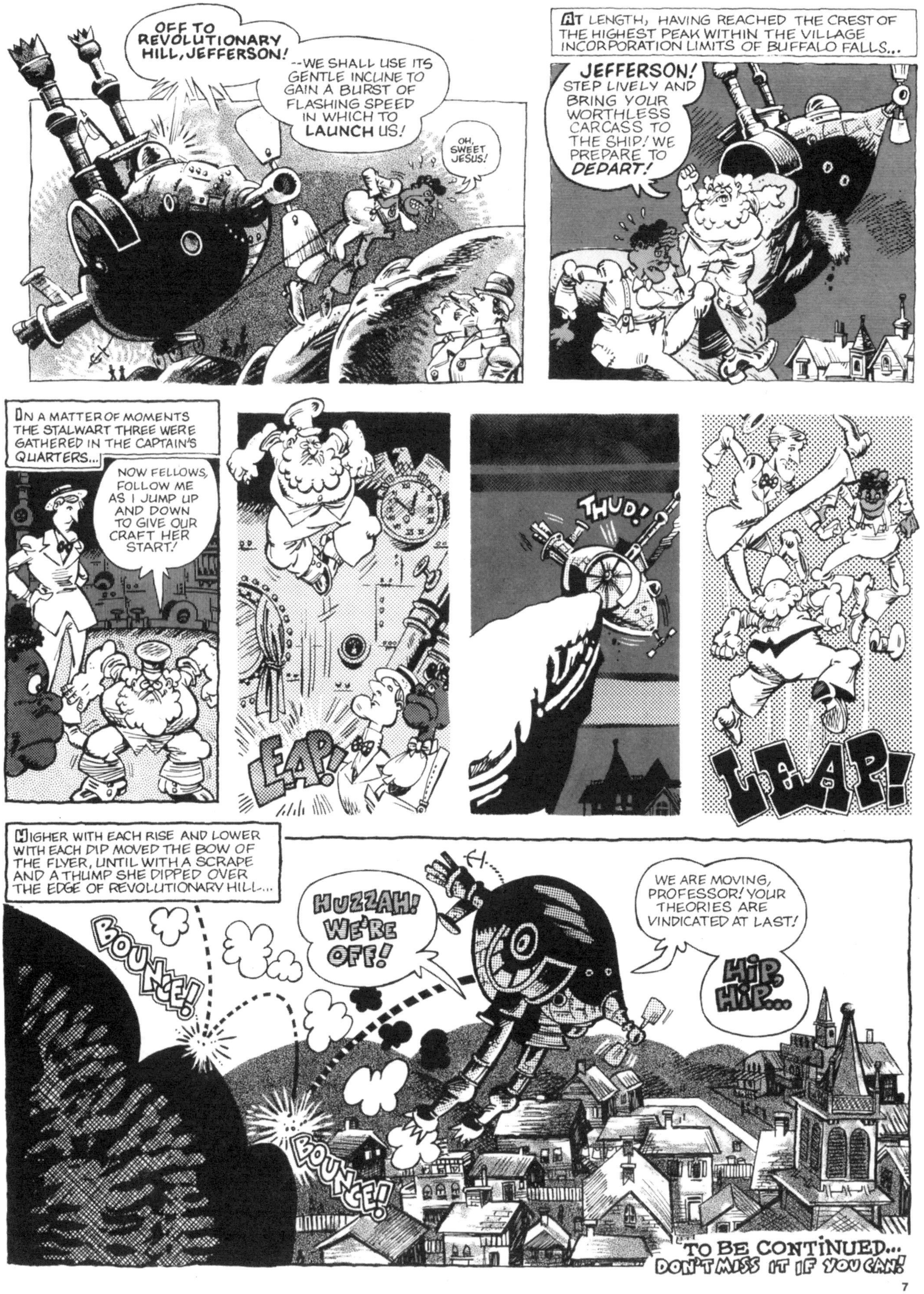

OFF TO REVOLUTIONARY HILL, JEFFERSON!
--WE SHALL USE ITS GENTLE INCLINE TO GAIN A BURST OF FLASHING SPEED IN WHICH TO LAUNCH US!
OH, SWEET JESUS!
AT LENGTH, HAVING REACHED THE CREST OF THE HIGHEST PEAK WITHIN THE VILLAGE INCORPORATION LIMITS OF BUFFALO FALLS...
JEFFERSON! STEP LIVELY AND BRING YOUR WORTHLESS CARCASS TO THE SHIP! WE PREPARE TO DEPART!
IN A MATTER OF MOMENTS THE STALWART THREE WERE GATHERED IN THE CAPTAIN'S QUARTERS...
NOW FELLOWS, FOLLOW ME AS I JUMP UP AND DOWN TO GIVE OUR CRAFT HER START!
LEAP!
THUD!
LEAP!
HIGHER WITH EACH RISE AND LOWER WITH EACH DIP MOVED THE BOW OF THE FLYER, UNTIL WITH A SCRAPE AND A THUMP SHE DIPPED OVER THE EDGE OF REVOLUTIONARY HILL...
BOUNCE!
HUZZAH! WE'RE OFF!
WE ARE MOVING, PROFESSOR! YOUR THEORIES ARE VINDICATED AT LAST!
HIP, HIP...
BOUNCE!
TO BE CONTINUED... DON'T MISS IT IF YOU CAN!

THE ADVENTURES OF PROFESSOR THINTWHISTLE

AND 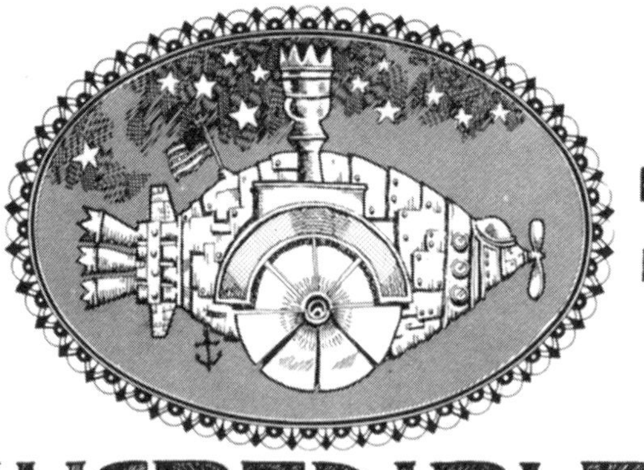 HIS

INCREDIBLE AETHER FLYER

STORY: DICK LUPOFF

ART: STEVE STILES

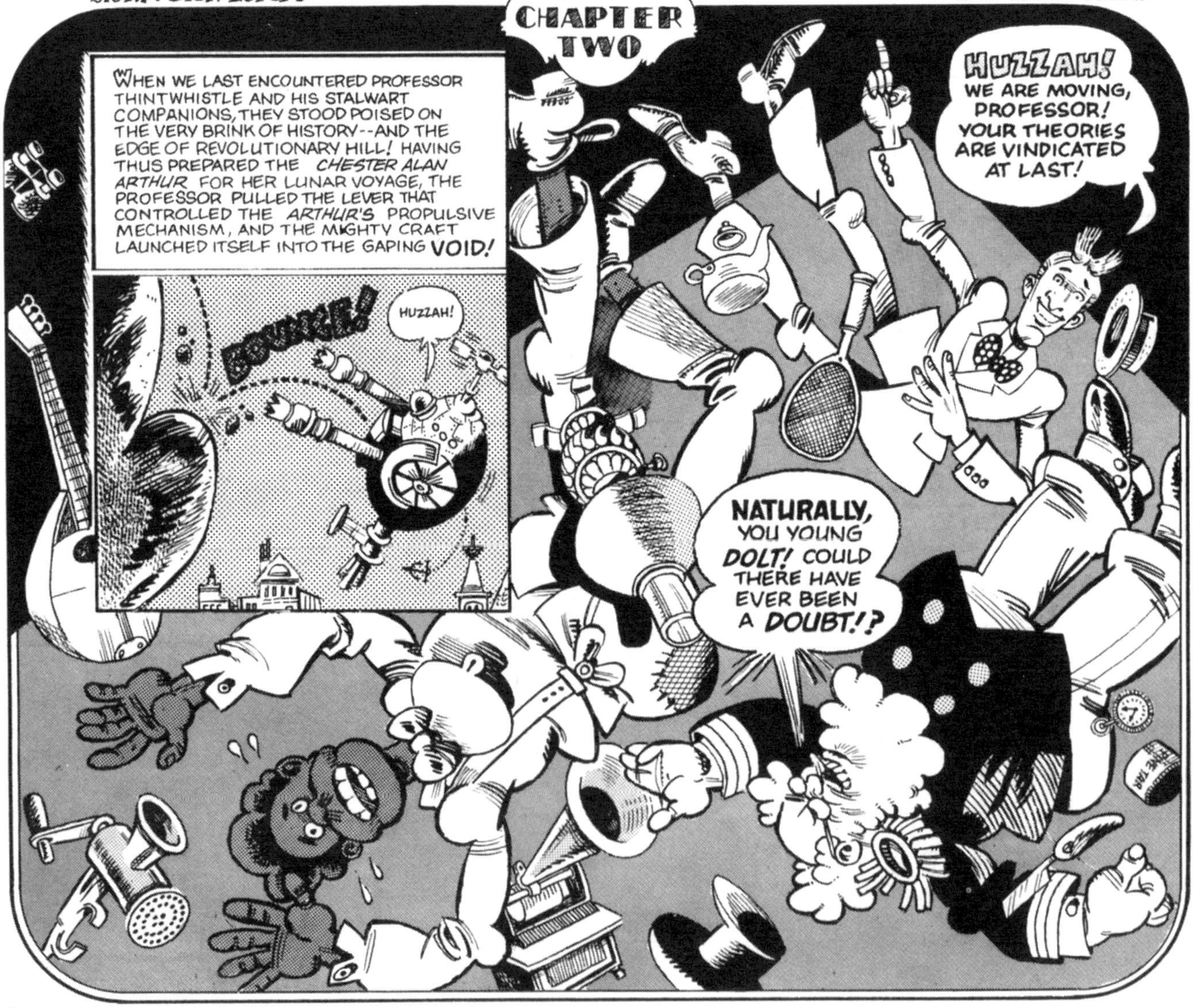
CHAPTER TWO
WHEN WE LAST ENCOUNTERED PROFESSOR THINTWHISTLE AND HIS STALWART COMPANIONS, THEY STOOD POISED ON THE VERY BRINK OF HISTORY--AND THE EDGE OF REVOLUTIONARY HILL! HAVING THUS PREPARED THE CHESTER ALAN ARTHUR FOR HER LUNAR VOYAGE, THE PROFESSOR PULLED THE LEVER THAT CONTROLLED THE ARTHUR'S PROPULSIVE MECHANISM, AND THE MIGHTY CRAFT LAUNCHED ITSELF INTO THE GAPING VOID!
BOUNCE!
HUZZAH!
HUZZAH! WE ARE MOVING, PROFESSOR! YOUR THEORIES ARE VINDICATED AT LAST!
NATURALLY, YOU YOUNG DOLT! COULD THERE HAVE EVER BEEN A DOUBT!?

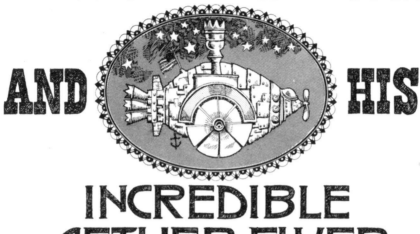

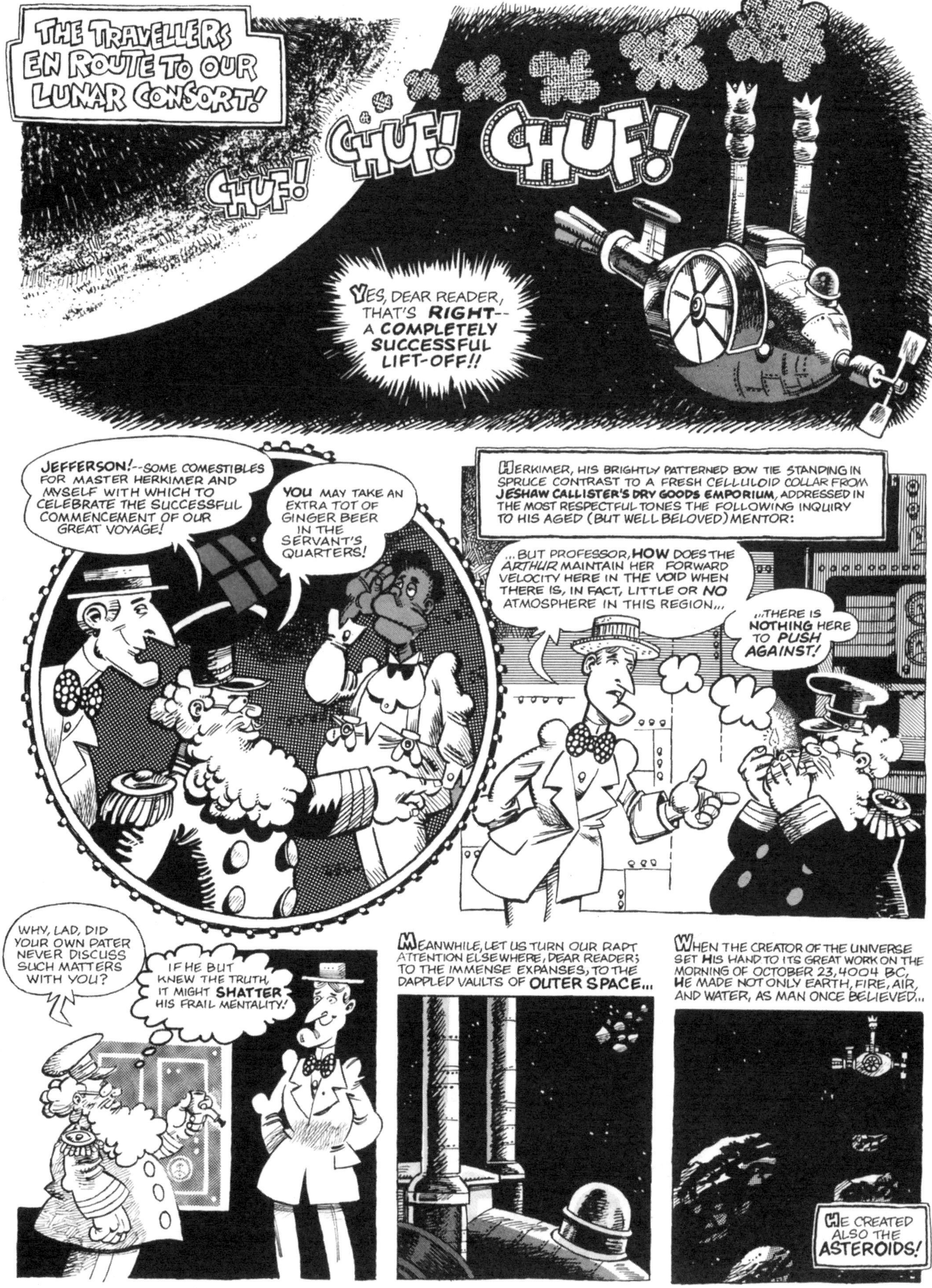

THE TRAVELLERS EN ROUTE TO OUR LUNAR CONSORT!
CHUF! CHUF! CHUF!
YES, DEAR READER, THAT'S RIGHT-- A COMPLETELY SUCCESSFUL LIFT-OFF!!
JEFFERSON!--SOME COMESTIBLES FOR MASTER HERKIMER AND MYSELF WITH WHICH TO CELEBRATE THE SUCCESSFUL COMMENCEMENT OF OUR GREAT VOYAGE!
YOU MAY TAKE AN EXTRA TOT OF GINGER BEER IN THE SERVANT'S QUARTERS!
HERKIMER, HIS BRIGHTLY PATTERNED BOW TIE STANDING IN SPRUCE CONTRAST TO A FRESH CELLULOID COLLAR FROM JESHAW CALLISTER'S DRY GOODS EMPORIUM, ADDRESSED IN THE MOST RESPECTFUL TONES THE FOLLOWING INQUIRY TO HIS AGED (BUT WELL BELOVED) MENTOR:
...BUT PROFESSOR, HOW DOES THE ARTHUR MAINTAIN HER FORWARD VELOCITY HERE IN THE VOID WHEN THERE IS, IN FACT, LITTLE OR NO ATMOSPHERE IN THIS REGION...
...THERE IS NOTHING HERE TO PUSH AGAINST!
WHY, LAD, DID YOUR OWN PATER NEVER DISCUSS SUCH MATTERS WITH YOU?
IF HE BUT KNEW THE TRUTH, IT MIGHT SHATTER HIS FRAIL MENTALITY!
MEANWHILE, LET US TURN OUR RAPT ATTENTION ELSEWHERE, DEAR READER; TO THE IMMENSE EXPANSES, TO THE DAPPLED VAULTS OF OUTER SPACE...
WHEN THE CREATOR OF THE UNIVERSE SET HIS HAND TO ITS GREAT WORK ON THE MORNING OF OCTOBER 23, 4004 BC, HE MADE NOT ONLY EARTH, FIRE, AIR, AND WATER, AS MAN ONCE BELIEVED...
HE CREATED ALSO THE ASTEROIDS!

THESE "CELESTIAL BODIES" ARE SOMETIMES THOUGHT TO BE THE PITIFUL **REMNANTS** OF SOME MIGHTY PLANET THAT ONCE EXISTED AT SOME ANCIENT TIME! PERHAPS DESTROYED BY NATURAL CAUSES OR **DIVINE INTERVENTION** -- OR PERHAPS BY THE **UNHOLY** APPLICATION OF KNOWLEDGE WROUGHT BY AN ERRING **SUPER-CIVILIZATION!!**

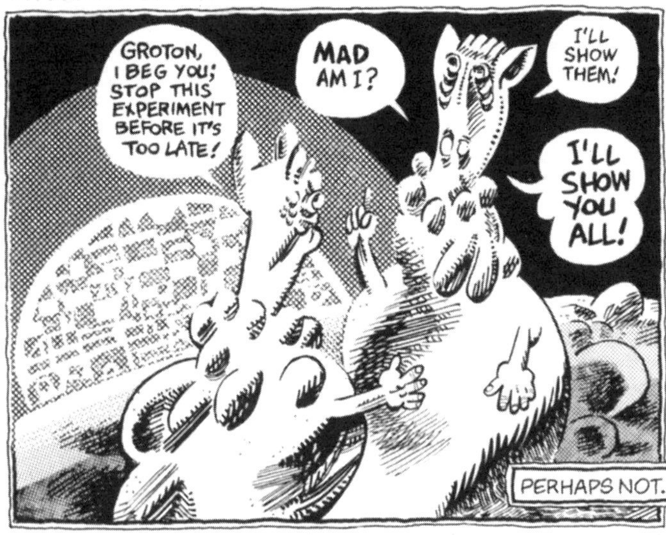
GROTON, I BEG YOU; STOP THIS EXPERIMENT BEFORE IT'S TOO LATE!
MAD AM I?
I'LL SHOW THEM!
I'LL SHOW YOU ALL!
PERHAPS NOT.

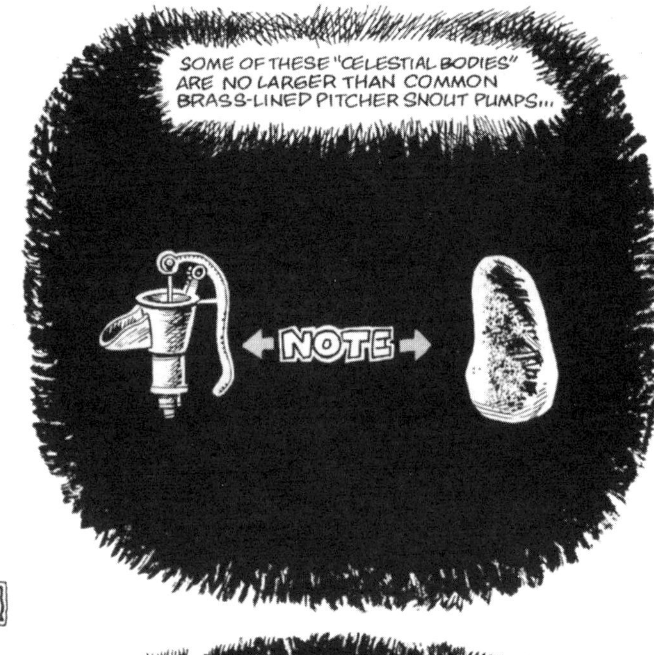
SOME OF THESE "CELESTIAL BODIES" ARE NO LARGER THAN COMMON BRASS-LINED PITCHER SNOUT PUMPS...
NOTE

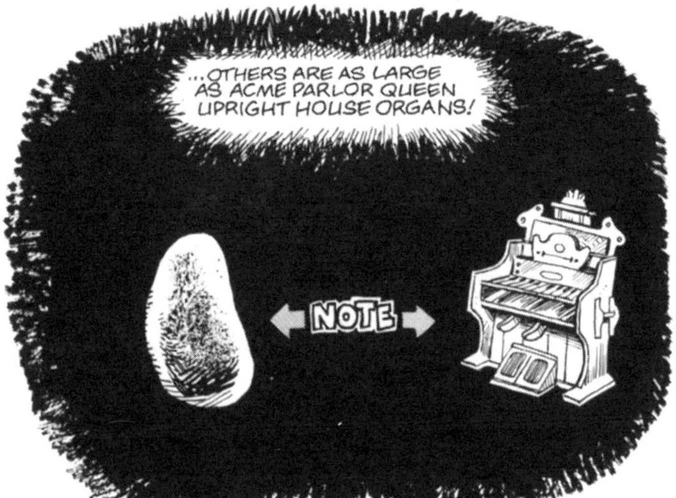
...OTHERS ARE AS LARGE AS ACME PARLOR QUEEN UPRIGHT HOUSE ORGANS!
NOTE

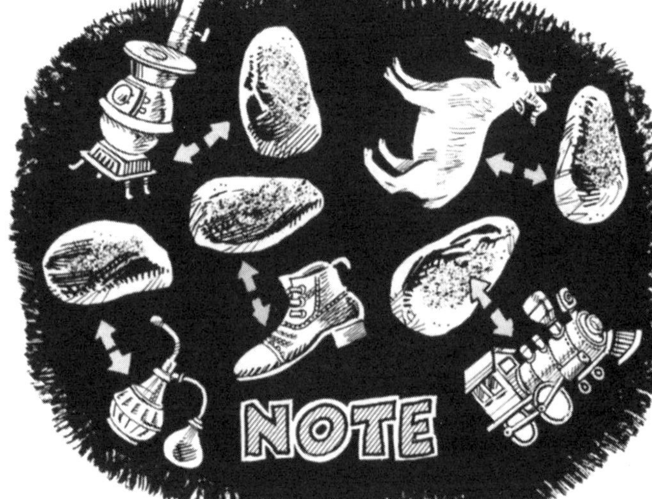
NOTE

ON ONE SUCH A MAMMOTH CELESTIAL BODY, AS IT WHIZZED THROUGH THE BLACK VOID THAT FILLS THE SPACE BETWEEN THE WORLDS, THERE WAS NOW ASSEMBLED A GATHERING OF MEN AND EQUIPMENT THAT WAS MOST LIKELY THE MOST **ODDLY ASSORTED** AND **REMARKABLE** EVER TO BE SEEN IN ONE SPOT! A SQUAD OF IMPERIAL **FRENCH GRENADIERS** STOOD ARRAYED WITH A GANG OF **ZULUS.** BESIDE THEM A UNIT OF TSARIST **COSSACKS;** WITH THEM A GRUMBLING CREW OF NAKED **CAVEMEN**, WIELDING WOODEN CLUBS AND STONE AXES. **PANZER** UNITS WITH THE DREAD **"COMMANCHE DRAGONS"** YOUTH CLUB OF YORKVILLE, MANHATTAN! **SAMURAI** AND **INCAS**, **GURKHAS** AND **LOBSTER BACKS**, ALL WERE ARRAYED IN FULL **BATTLE DRESS**, BEARING EQUIPMENT OF **WAR!**

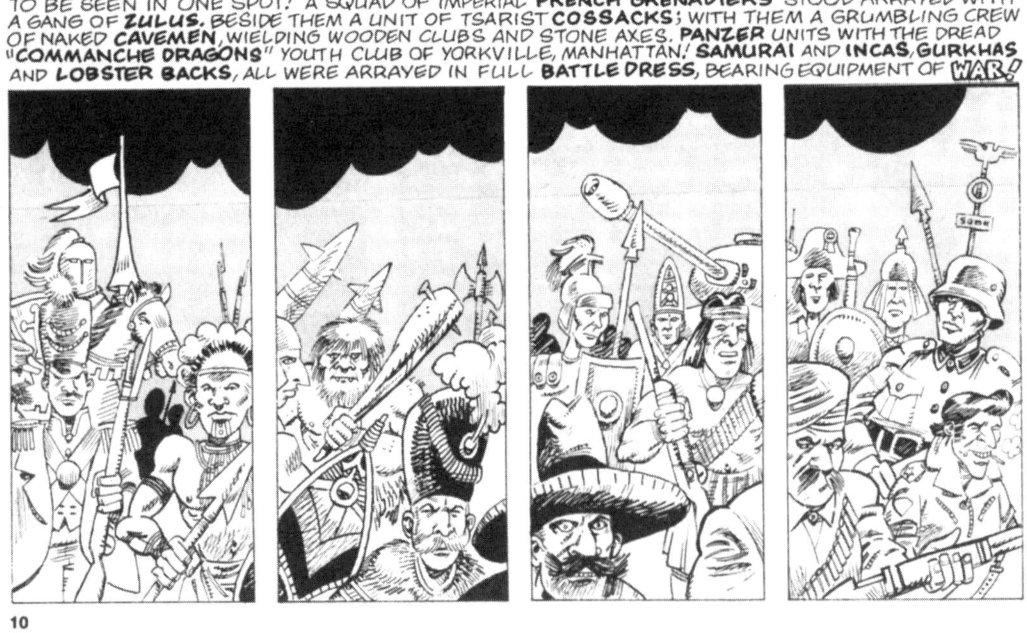

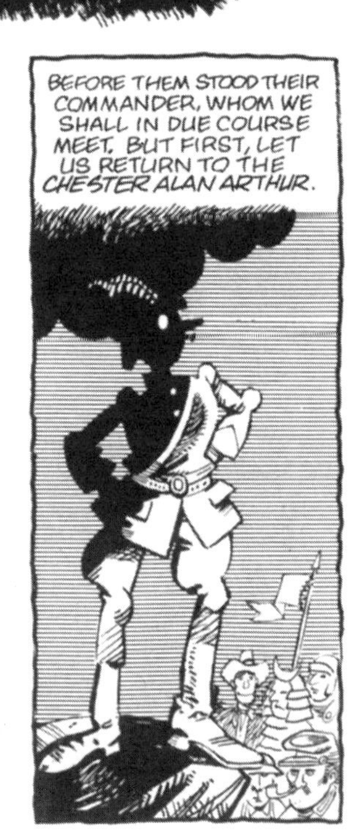
BEFORE THEM STOOD THEIR COMMANDER, WHOM WE SHALL IN DUE COURSE MEET. BUT FIRST, LET US RETURN TO THE *CHESTER ALAN ARTHUR*.

... AND SO YOU SEE, DEAR BOY, AS LONG AS OUR SUPPLY OF STOUT BITUMINOUS COAL REMAINS, WE HAVE NAUGHT TO FEAR FOR HAVING NAUGHT TO PUSH AGAINST!
SEE?
O JUPITER OF MIND!
O AUGUSTINE OF SOUL!
WHILE THE PROFESSOR LUBRICATES THE CRANIUM OF HERKIMER WITH THE WONDERS OF PHYSICAL PHILOSOPHY, PERFIDY THREATENS!
LET THOSE TWO MEANDER ON! I'VE MORE IMPORTANT MATTERS TO ATTEND TO!
IT IS NONE OTHER THAN JEFFERSON JACKSON CLAY! HAVING SOLIDLY BOLTED THE HATCHWAY LEADING TO THE SERVANTS QUARTERS, THE DUSKY AFRICAN HAD REMOVED FROM A PLACE OF CONCEALMENT A SINISTER HELMET OF RATHER UNUSUAL DESIGN, CLAMPING IT FIRMLY TO HIS FUZZY POLL!
A CURLING INSULATED WIRE LED FROM THE HELMET TO A PANEL OF INSTRUMENTS REVEALED WITH THE UNLOCKING OF A RUN-DOWN, SECONDHAND ROLLTOP DESK...
HMM... OHMMETER NEEDS PRECISION CALIBRATION...
RHEOSTAT CONTROL SECTION COMPLETED...
CARRIER WAVE FOR COMPENSATION COUNTER BALANCER IN PLACE...
POLARITY REVERSAL FIELD OPERATION COMPLETION CORRELATED!
AND THEN, AS THE VALIANT LITTLE CRAFT BEARING THE THREE BUFFALO FALLSIANS CHUFFED BRAVELY THROUGH THE EMPTINESS OF THE OUTER EXPANSES, THE DRAWLING AND SLOVENLY VOICE OF THE BLACKAMOOR, NOW TRAINED TO A TOTALLY UNEXPECTED CRISPNESS, CRACKLED MENACINGLY THROUGH THE AETHER...
UF CHUF CHUF
AGENT CLAY TO ASTEROID ARMY!
AGENT CLAY TO DOOM ASTEROID!
OVER!
DO YOU READ ME?

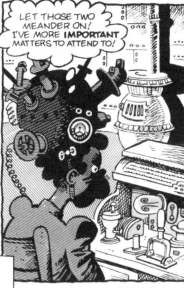

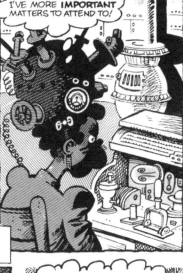

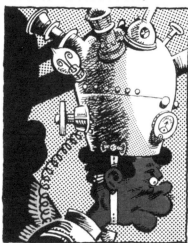

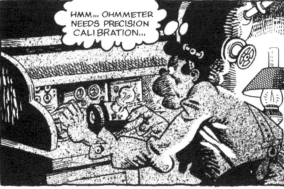

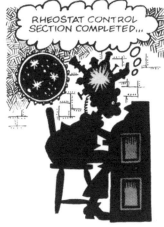

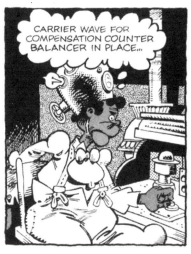

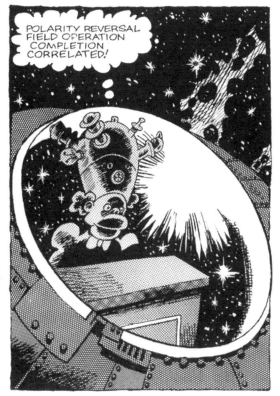

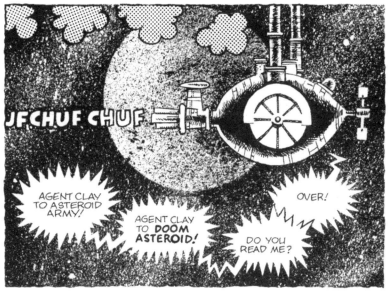

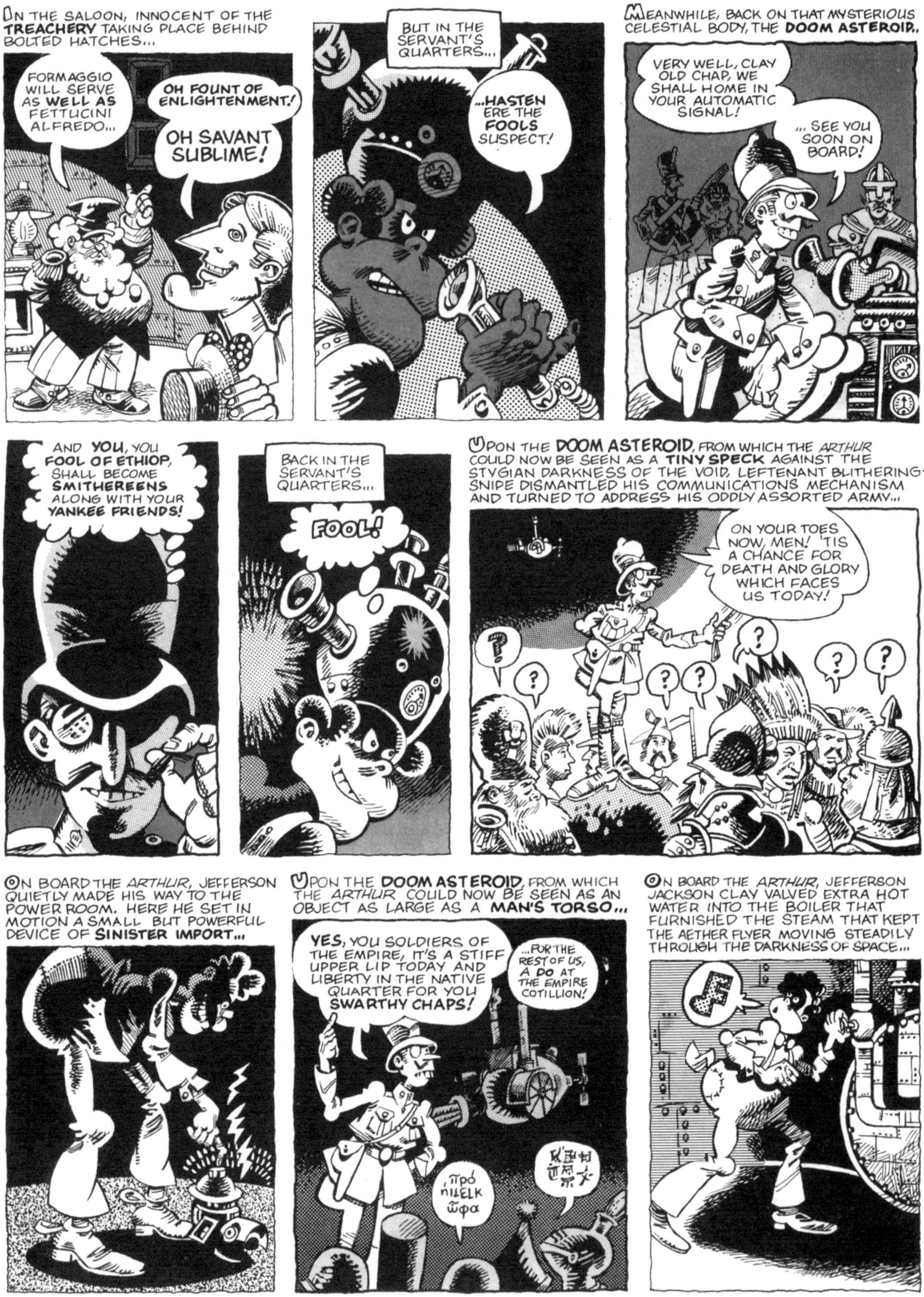
ON THE SALOON, INNOCENT OF THE TREACHERY TAKING PLACE BEHIND BOLTED HATCHES...
FORMAGGIO WILL SERVE AS WELL AS FETTUCINI ALFREDO...
OH FOUNT OF ENLIGHTENMENT!
OH SAVANT SUBLIME!
BUT IN THE SERVANT'S QUARTERS...
...HASTEN ERE THE FOOLS SUSPECT!
MEANWHILE, BACK ON THAT MYSTERIOUS CELESTIAL BODY, THE DOOM ASTEROID..
VERY WELL, CLAY OLD CHAP, WE SHALL HOME IN YOUR AUTOMATIC SIGNAL!
...SEE YOU SOON ON BOARD!
AND YOU, YOU FOOL OF ETHIOP, SHALL BECOME SMITHEREENS ALONG WITH YOUR YANKEE FRIENDS!
BACK IN THE SERVANT'S QUARTERS...
FOOL!
UPON THE DOOM ASTEROID, FROM WHICH THE ARTHUR COULD NOW BE SEEN AS A TINY SPECK AGAINST THE STYGIAN DARKNESS OF THE VOID, LEFTENANT BLITHERING-SNIPE DISMANTLED HIS COMMUNICATIONS MECHANISM AND TURNED TO ADDRESS HIS ODDLY ASSORTED ARMY...
ON YOUR TOES NOW, MEN! 'TIS A CHANCE FOR DEATH AND GLORY WHICH FACES US TODAY!
?
ON BOARD THE ARTHUR, JEFFERSON QUIETLY MADE HIS WAY TO THE POWER ROOM. HERE HE SET IN MOTION A SMALL BUT POWERFUL DEVICE OF SINISTER IMPORT...
UPON THE DOOM ASTEROID, FROM WHICH THE ARTHUR COULD NOW BE SEEN AS AN OBJECT AS LARGE AS A MAN'S TORSO...
YES, YOU SOLDIERS OF THE EMPIRE, IT'S A STIFF UPPER LIP TODAY AND LIBERTY IN THE NATIVE QUARTER FOR YOU SWARTHY CHAPS!
...FOR THE REST OF US, A DO AT THE EMPIRE COTILLION!
ON BOARD THE ARTHUR, JEFFERSON JACKSON CLAY VALVED EXTRA HOT WATER INTO THE BOILER THAT FURNISHED THE STEAM THAT KEPT THE AETHER FLYER MOVING STEADILY THROUGH THE DARKNESS OF SPACE...
F

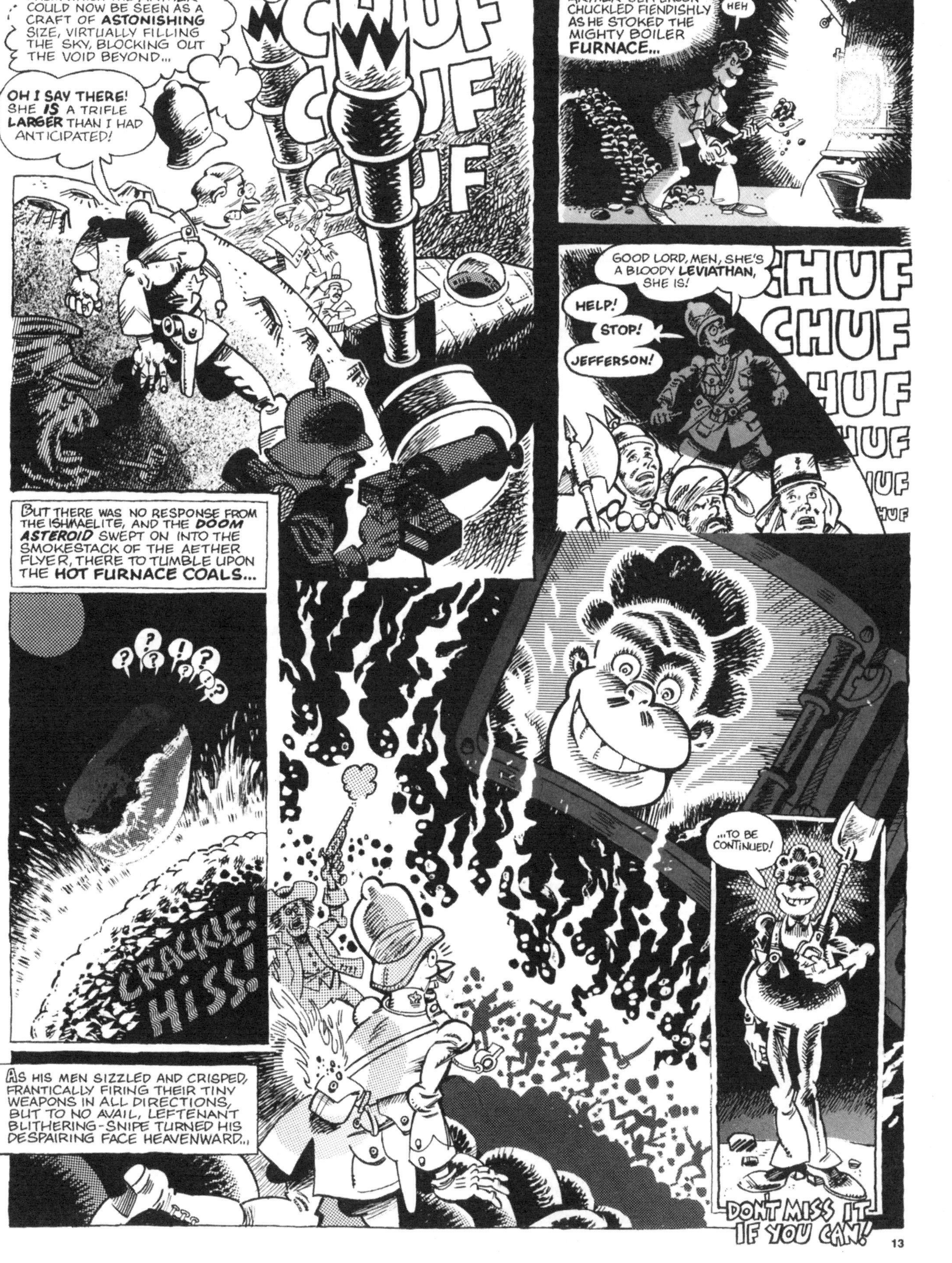

UPON THE DOOM ASTEROID, FROM WHICH THE ARTHUR COULD NOW BE SEEN AS A CRAFT OF ASTONISHING SIZE, VIRTUALLY FILLING THE SKY, BLOCKING OUT THE VOID BEYOND...
CHUF CHUF CHUF
OH I SAY THERE! SHE IS A TRIFLE LARGER THAN I HAD ANTICIPATED!
ON BOARD THE ARTHUR JEFFERSON CHUCKLED FIENDISHLY AS HE STOKED THE MIGHTY BOILER FURNACE...
HEH
HEH
HEH
GOOD LORD, MEN, SHE'S A BLOODY LEVIATHAN, SHE IS!
HELP!
STOP!
JEFFERSON!
CHUF CHUF CHUF CHUF CHUF CHUF
BUT THERE WAS NO RESPONSE FROM THE ISHMAELITE, AND THE DOOM ASTEROID SWEPT ON INTO THE SMOKESTACK OF THE AETHER FLYER, THERE TO TUMBLE UPON THE HOT FURNACE COALS...
? ? ! ? ? ? ?
CRACKLE! HISS!
AS HIS MEN SIZZLED AND CRISPED, FRANTICALLY FIRING THEIR TINY WEAPONS IN ALL DIRECTIONS, BUT TO NO AVAIL, LEFTENANT BLITHERING-SNIPE TURNED HIS DESPAIRING FACE HEAVENWARD...
...TO BE CONTINUED!
DON'T MISS IT IF YOU CAN!

THE ADVENTURES OF PROFESSOR THINTWHISTLE AND HIS INCREDIBLE AETHER FLYER

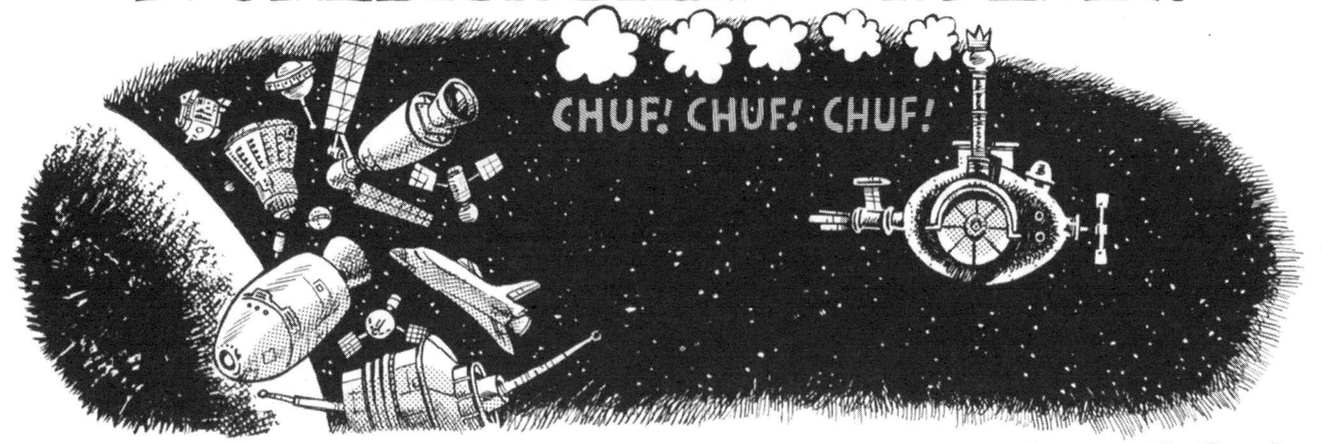
CHUF! CHUF! CHUF!

CHAPTER THREE: LAND HO!

DICK LUPOFF

STEVE STILES

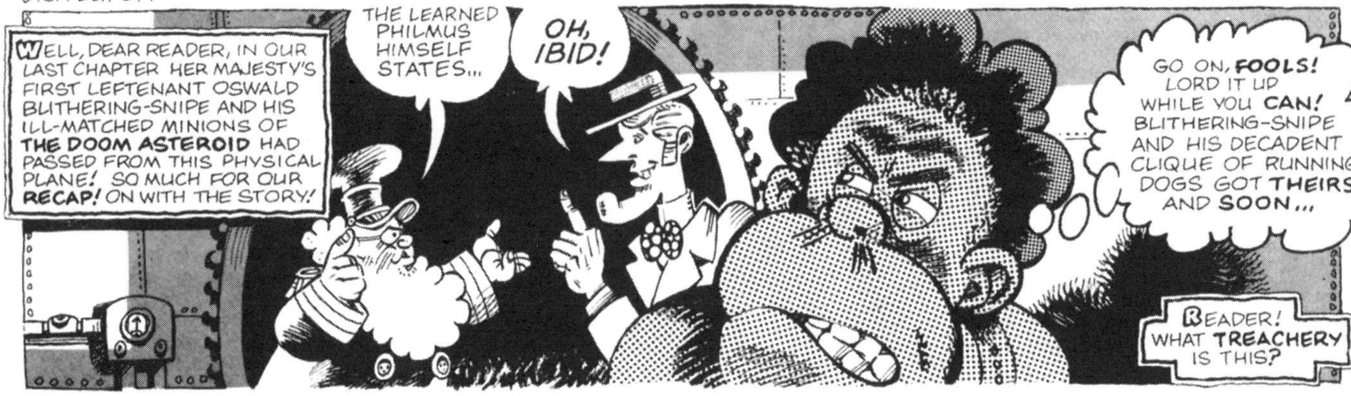
WELL, DEAR READER, IN OUR LAST CHAPTER HER MAJESTY'S FIRST LEFTENANT OSWALD BLITHERING-SNIPE AND HIS ILL-MATCHED MINIONS OF **THE DOOM ASTEROID** HAD PASSED FROM THIS PHYSICAL PLANE! SO MUCH FOR OUR **RECAP!** ON WITH THE STORY!
THE LEARNED PHILMUS HIMSELF STATES...
OH, IBID!
GO ON, **FOOLS!** LORD IT UP WHILE YOU **CAN!** BLITHERING-SNIPE AND HIS DECADENT CLIQUE OF RUNNING DOGS GOT **THEIRS!** AND **SOON...**
READER! WHAT **TREACHERY** IS THIS?

WHAT STRANGE AND PERVERSE SENSE OF DISLOYALTY **SENDS** THE BLACKAMOOR'S SIMPLE INTELLECT DOWN SUCH A PATH?

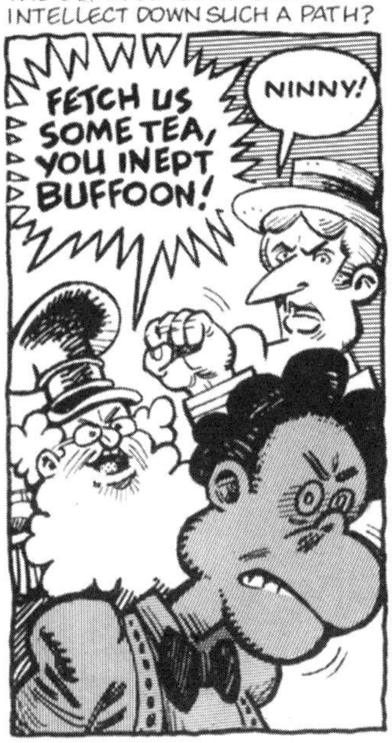
FETCH US SOME TEA, YOU INEPT BUFFOON!
NINNY!

LET US SKIP AHEAD IN TIME, PASSING OVER DAYS OF SHIP-BOARD ROUTINE. UPON THE CAPTAIN'S VERANDA WE FIND **THEOBALD URIAH THINTWHISTLE** SEDULOUSLY EXAMINING A VARIETY OF COMPLEX KNOBS, VALVES, CONTROLS, SWITCHES...

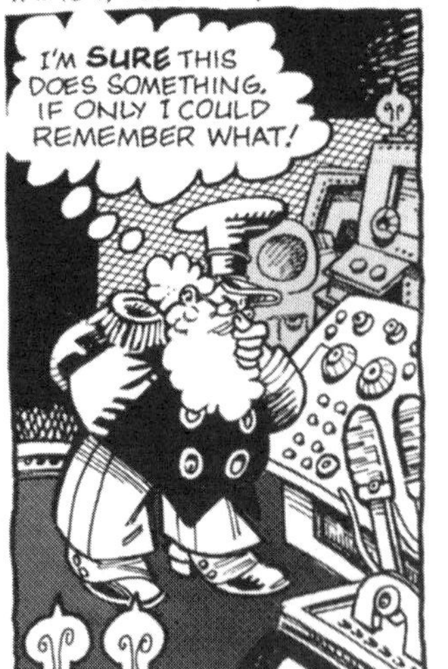
I'M **SURE** THIS DOES SOMETHING. IF ONLY I COULD REMEMBER WHAT!

AT THE REAR OF THE CAPTAIN'S VERANDA CAN BE SEEN THE WILY **JEFFERSON JACKSON CLAY,** HEFTING A BROOM IN HIS CUSTOMARY **LACKADAISICAL** MANNER. FROM HIS LIPS THERE RISES A SIMPLE TUNE, SYNCO-PATED IN THE NATURAL RHYTHM WITH WHICH A JUST NATURE COMPENSATES LESSER RACES...

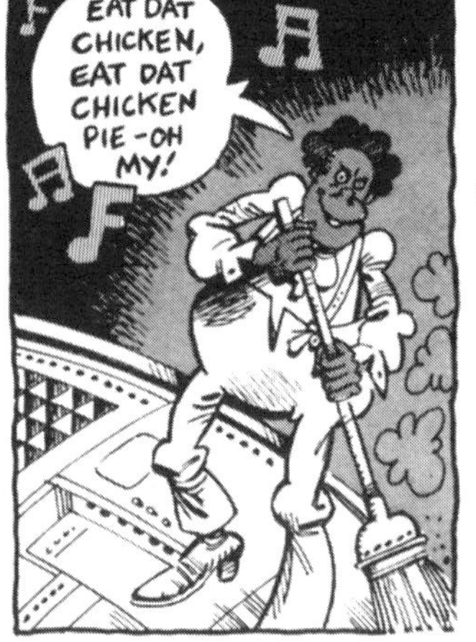
EAT DAT CHICKEN, EAT DAT CHICKEN PIE-OH MY!

AND BENEATH THE INNOCENT ORBS OF **HERKIMER** THERE PASSES LEWD ROTOGRAVURES, PORTRAITS OF "LADIES" (!) IN IMMODEST STATES OF **DISROBE-MENT!** BLAME NOT THE LAD; BLAME INSTEAD THE **EXPLOITERS OF YOUTH** FOR PUBLISHING PICTURES WITH SUCH TITLES AS "A BRACE OF HEART BREAKERS," OR "WHY THE SCARECROW RAN AWAY FROM THE FARM"!

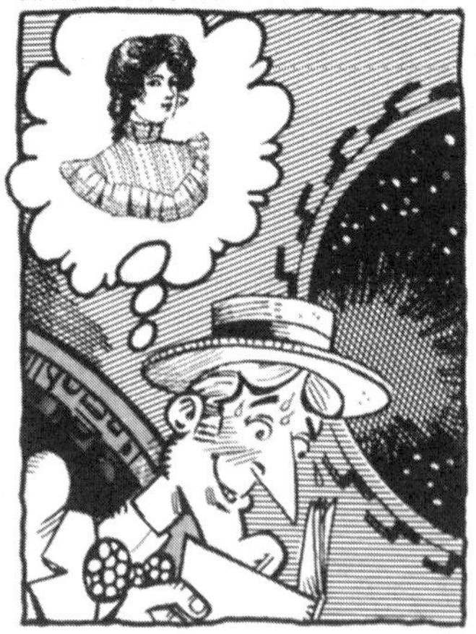

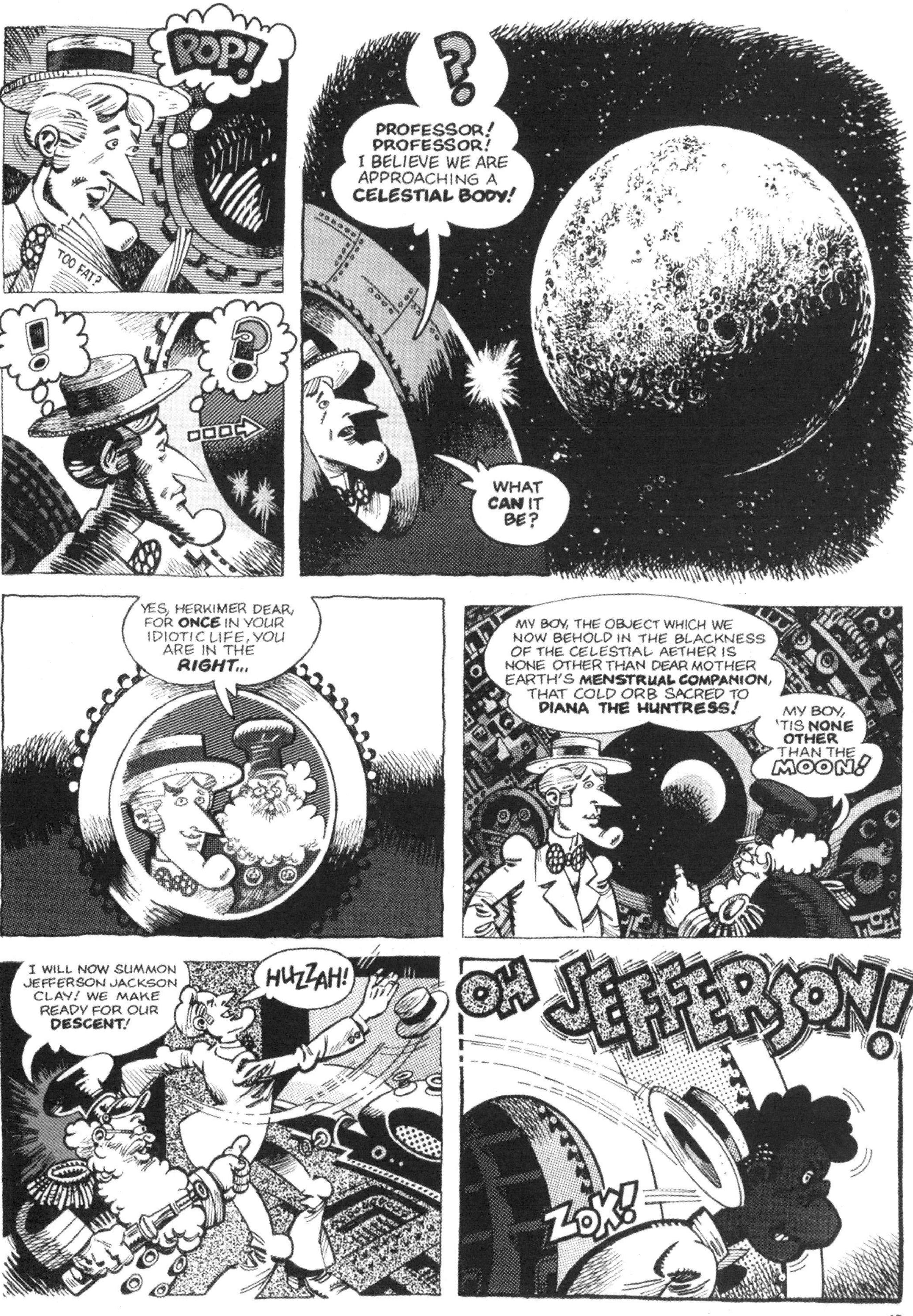
POP!
TOO FAT?
?
PROFESSOR! PROFESSOR! I BELIEVE WE ARE APPROACHING A CELESTIAL BODY!
!
?
WHAT CAN IT BE?
YES, HERKIMER DEAR, FOR ONCE IN YOUR IDIOTIC LIFE, YOU ARE IN THE RIGHT...
MY BOY, THE OBJECT WHICH WE NOW BEHOLD IN THE BLACKNESS OF THE CELESTIAL AETHER IS NONE OTHER THAN DEAR MOTHER EARTH'S MENSTRUAL COMPANION, THAT COLD ORB SACRED TO DIANA THE HUNTRESS!
MY BOY, 'TIS NONE OTHER THAN THE MOON!
I WILL NOW SUMMON JEFFERSON JACKSON CLAY! WE MAKE READY FOR OUR DESCENT!
HUZZAH!
OH JEFFERSON!
ZOK!

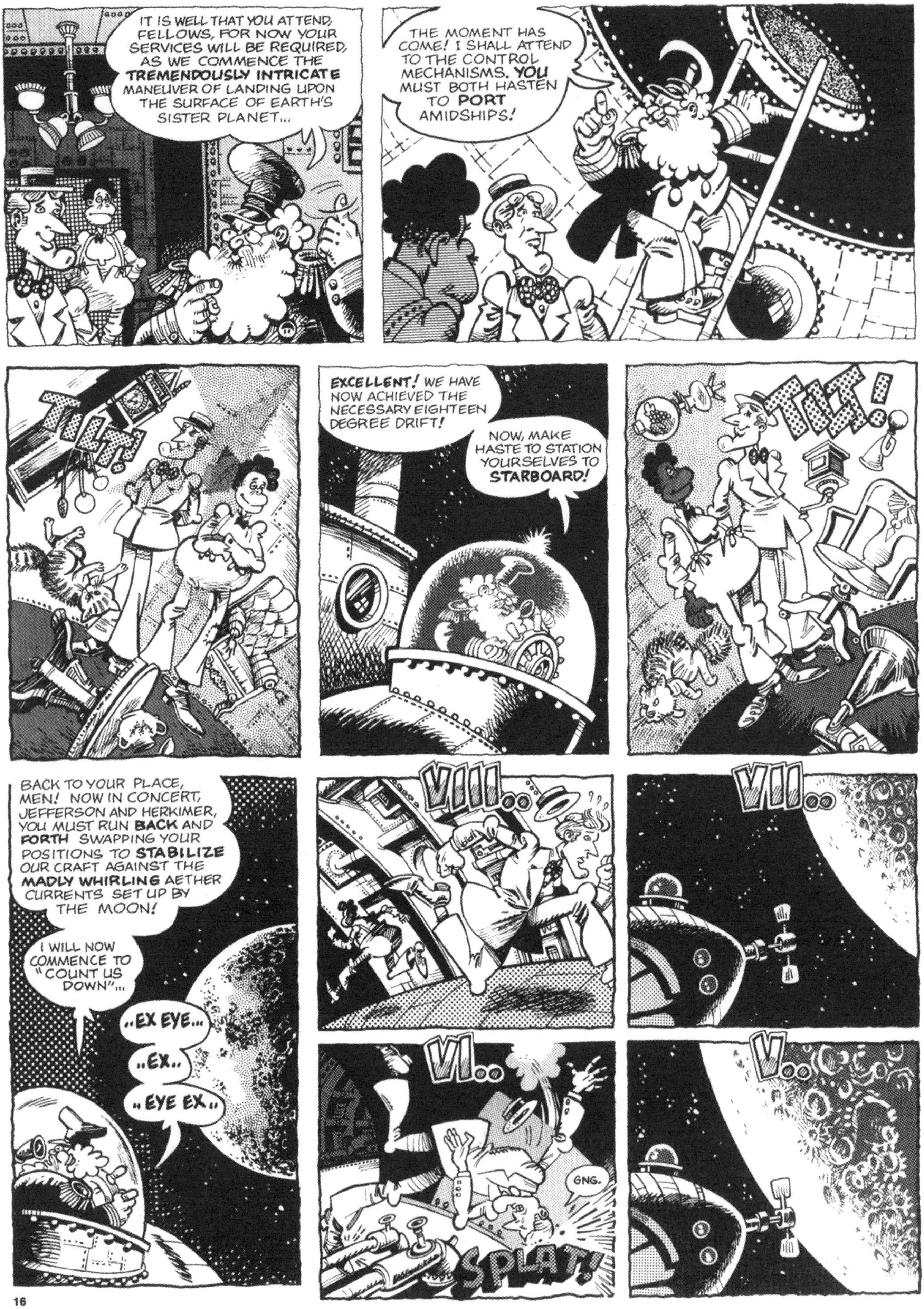

IT IS WELL THAT YOU ATTEND, FELLOWS, FOR NOW YOUR SERVICES WILL BE REQUIRED, AS WE COMMENCE THE TREMENDOUSLY INTRICATE MANEUVER OF LANDING UPON THE SURFACE OF EARTH'S SISTER PLANET...
THE MOMENT HAS COME! I SHALL ATTEND TO THE CONTROL MECHANISMS. YOU MUST BOTH HASTEN TO PORT AMIDSHIPS!
TILT!
EXCELLENT! WE HAVE NOW ACHIEVED THE NECESSARY EIGHTEEN DEGREE DRIFT!
NOW, MAKE HASTE TO STATION YOURSELVES TO STARBOARD!
TILT!
BACK TO YOUR PLACE, MEN! NOW IN CONCERT, JEFFERSON AND HERKIMER, YOU MUST RUN BACK AND FORTH SWAPPING YOUR POSITIONS TO STABILIZE OUR CRAFT AGAINST THE MADLY WHIRLING AETHER CURRENTS SET UP BY THE MOON!
I WILL NOW COMMENCE TO "COUNT US DOWN"...
..EX EYE...
..EX..
..EYE EX..
VIII..
VII..
VI..
GNG.
SPLAT!
V..

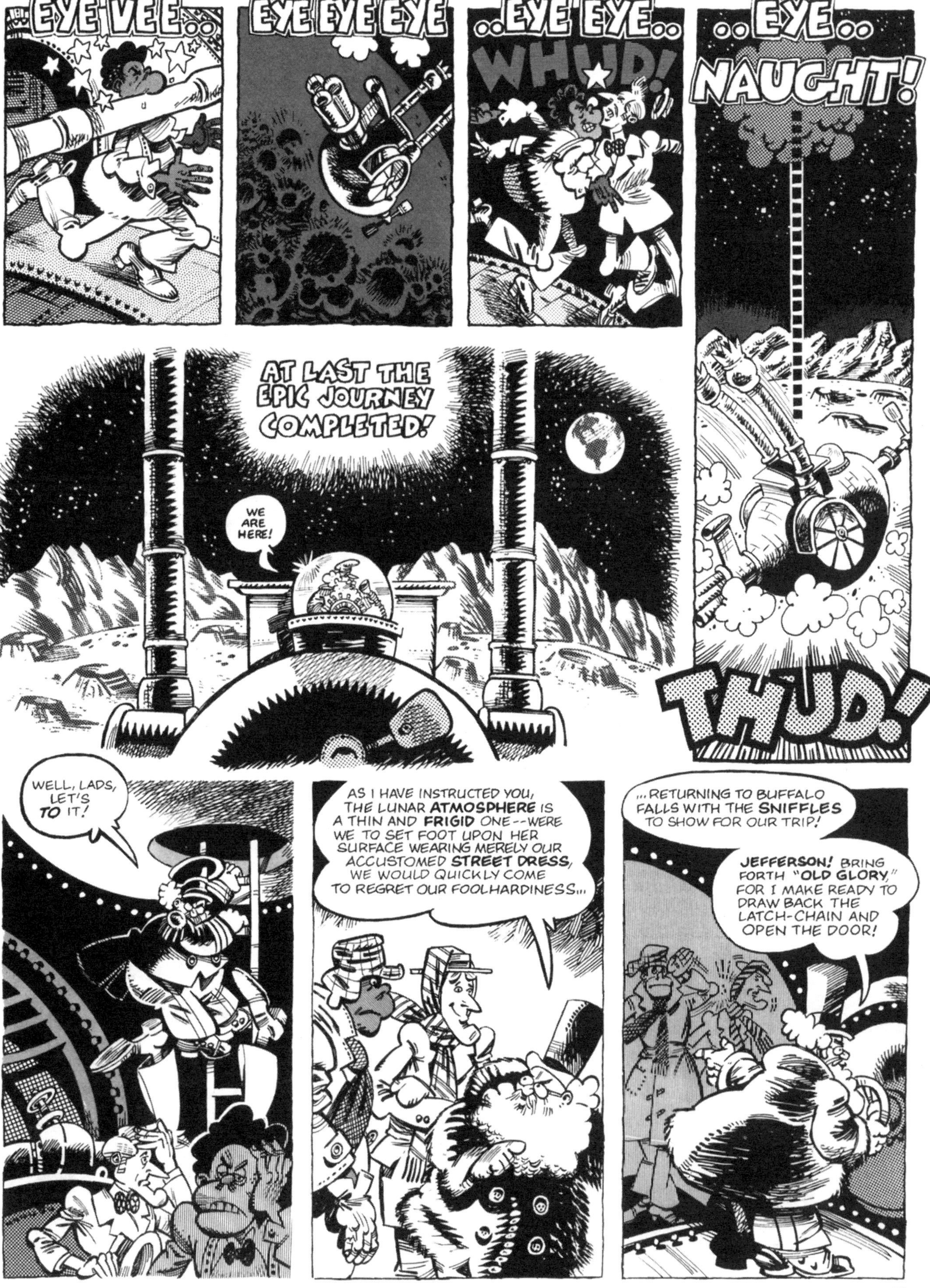
EYE VEE E..
EYE EYE EYE
..EYE EYE..
WHUD!
..EYE..
NAUGHT!
AT LAST THE EPIC JOURNEY COMPLETED!
WE ARE HERE!
THUD!
WELL, LADS, LET'S TO IT!
AS I HAVE INSTRUCTED YOU, THE LUNAR ATMOSPHERE IS A THIN AND FRIGID ONE--WERE WE TO SET FOOT UPON HER SURFACE WEARING MERELY OUR ACCUSTOMED STREET DRESS, WE WOULD QUICKLY COME TO REGRET OUR FOOLHARDINESS...
...RETURNING TO BUFFALO FALLS WITH THE SNIFFLES TO SHOW FOR OUR TRIP!
JEFFERSON! BRING FORTH "OLD GLORY," FOR I MAKE READY TO DRAW BACK THE LATCH-CHAIN AND OPEN THE DOOR!

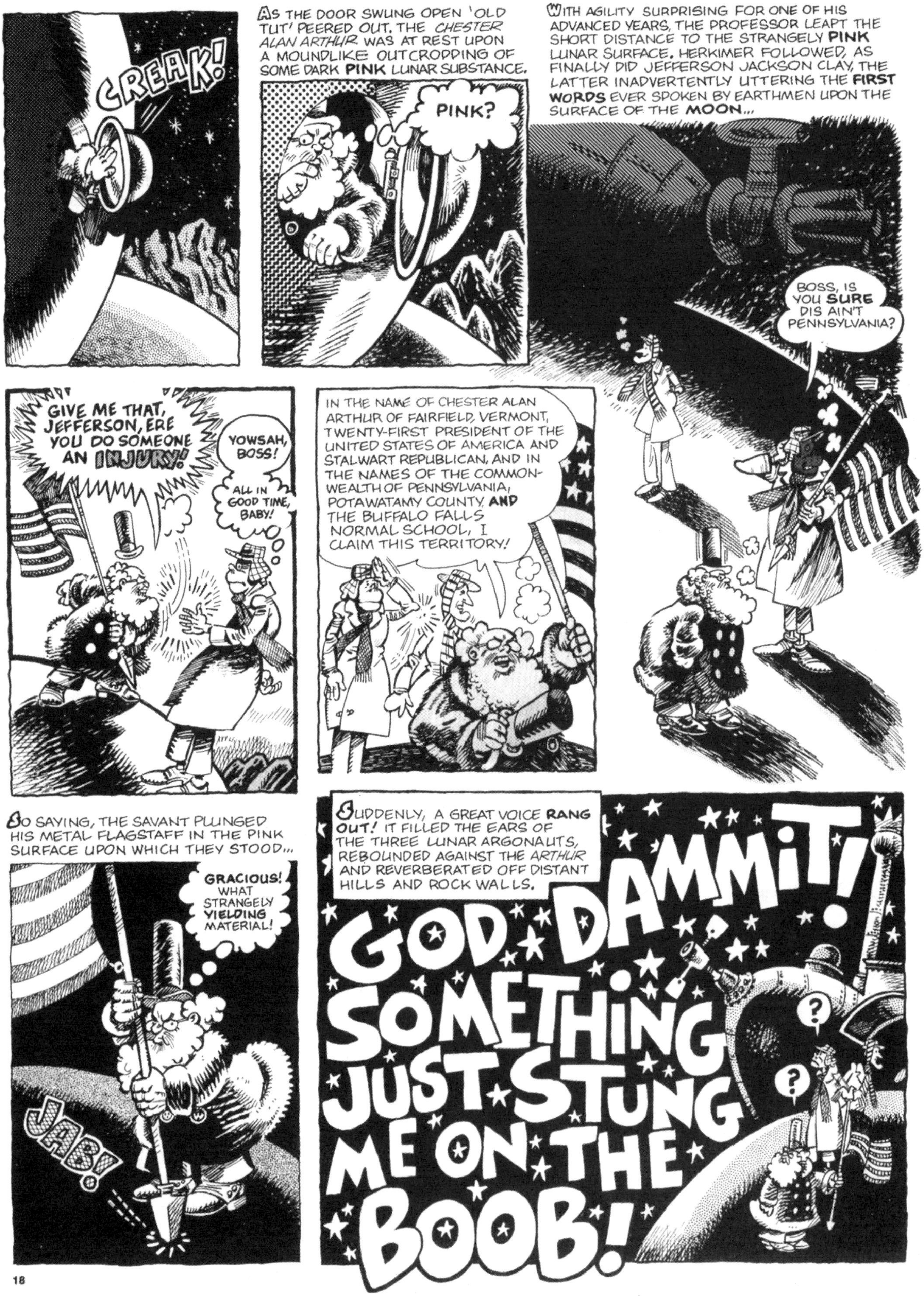
CREAK!
AS THE DOOR SWUNG OPEN 'OLD TUT' PEERED OUT. THE CHESTER ALAN ARTHUR WAS AT REST UPON A MOUNDLIKE OUTCROPPING OF SOME DARK PINK LUNAR SUBSTANCE.
PINK?
WITH AGILITY SURPRISING FOR ONE OF HIS ADVANCED YEARS, THE PROFESSOR LEAPT THE SHORT DISTANCE TO THE STRANGELY PINK LUNAR SURFACE. HERKIMER FOLLOWED, AS FINALLY DID JEFFERSON JACKSON CLAY, THE LATTER INADVERTENTLY UTTERING THE FIRST WORDS EVER SPOKEN BY EARTHMEN UPON THE SURFACE OF THE MOON...
BOSS, IS YOU SURE DIS AIN'T PENNSYLVANIA?
GIVE ME THAT, JEFFERSON, ERE YOU DO SOMEONE AN INJURY!
YOWSAH, BOSS!
ALL IN GOOD TIME, BABY!
IN THE NAME OF CHESTER ALAN ARTHUR OF FAIRFIELD, VERMONT, TWENTY-FIRST PRESIDENT OF THE UNITED STATES OF AMERICA AND STALWART REPUBLICAN, AND IN THE NAMES OF THE COMMONWEALTH OF PENNSYLVANIA, POTAWATAMY COUNTY, AND THE BUFFALO FALLS NORMAL SCHOOL, I CLAIM THIS TERRITORY!
SO SAYING, THE SAVANT PLUNGED HIS METAL FLAGSTAFF IN THE PINK SURFACE UPON WHICH THEY STOOD...
GRACIOUS! WHAT STRANGELY YIELDING MATERIAL!
JAB!
SUDDENLY, A GREAT VOICE RANG OUT! IT FILLED THE EARS OF THE THREE LUNAR ARGONAUTS, REBOUNDED AGAINST THE ARTHUR AND REVERBERATED OFF DISTANT HILLS AND ROCK WALLS.
GOD DAMMIT! SOMETHING JUST STUNG ME ON THE BOOB!
?
?

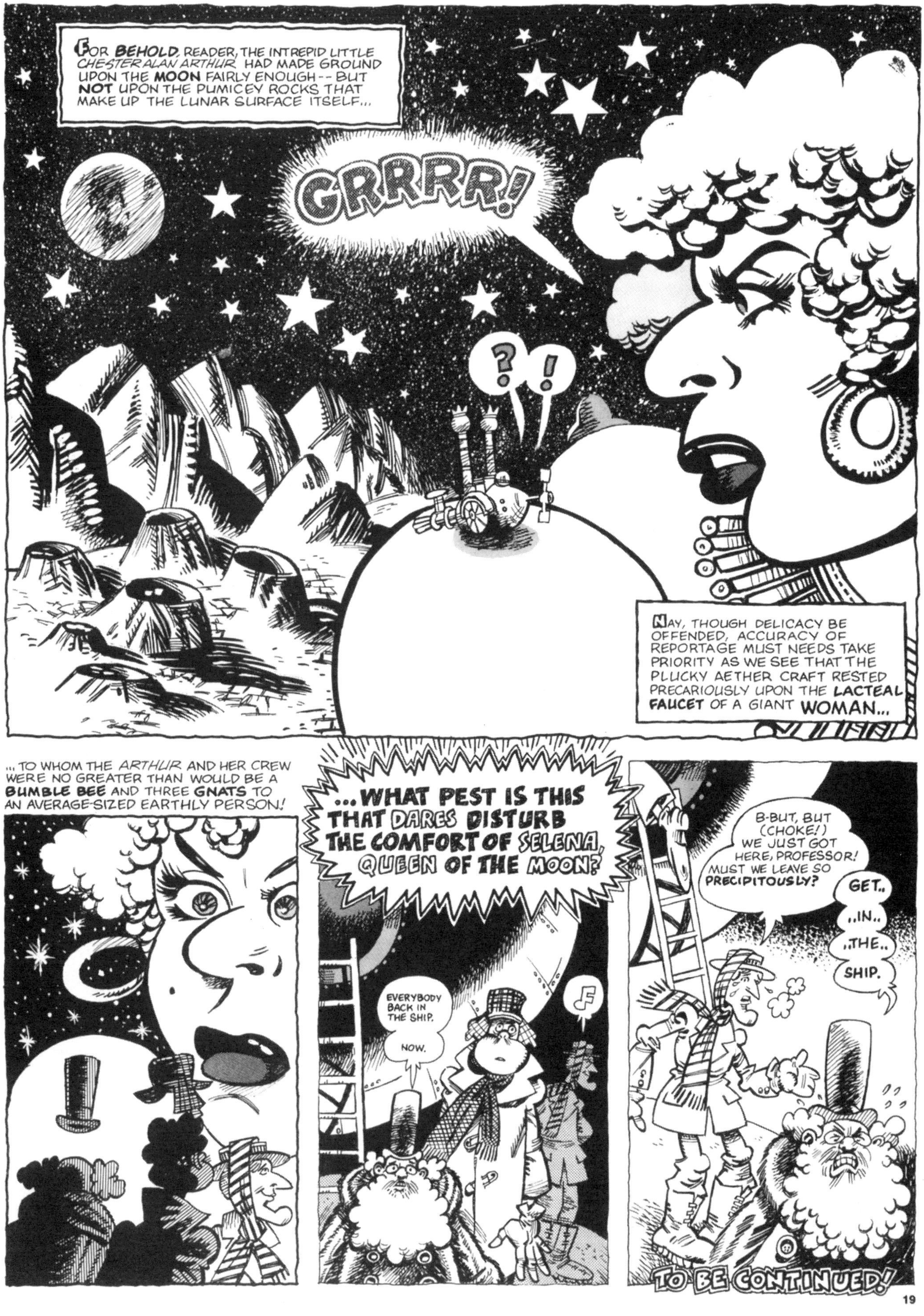
FOR BEHOLD, READER, THE INTREPID LITTLE CHESTER ALAN ARTHUR HAD MADE GROUND UPON THE MOON FAIRLY ENOUGH -- BUT NOT UPON THE PUMICEY ROCKS THAT MAKE UP THE LUNAR SURFACE ITSELF...
GRRRR!
?
!
NAY, THOUGH DELICACY BE OFFENDED, ACCURACY OF REPORTAGE MUST NEEDS TAKE PRIORITY AS WE SEE THAT THE PLUCKY AETHER CRAFT RESTED PRECARIOUSLY UPON THE LACTEAL FAUCET OF A GIANT WOMAN...
...TO WHOM THE ARTHUR AND HER CREW WERE NO GREATER THAN WOULD BE A BUMBLE BEE AND THREE GNATS TO AN AVERAGE-SIZED EARTHLY PERSON!
...WHAT PEST IS THIS THAT DARES DISTURB THE COMFORT OF SELENA, QUEEN OF THE MOON?
EVERYBODY BACK IN THE SHIP.
NOW.
B-BUT, BUT (CHOKE!) WE JUST GOT HERE, PROFESSOR! MUST WE LEAVE SO PRECIPITOUSLY?
GET.. ..IN.. ..THE.. SHIP.
TO BE CONTINUED!

THE ADVENTURES OF PROFESSOR THINTWHISTLE AND HIS INCREDIBLE AETHER FLYER

CHAPTER FOUR: SOME SURPRISES

BEHOLD, READER, THE DAUNTLESS LITTLE *CHESTER ALAN ARTHUR* HAD DESCENDED UPON THE **MOON** FAIRLY ENOUGH-- HOWEVER, THE SPUNKY, STEAM-DRIVEN CRAFT RESTED PRECARIOUSLY UPON THE LACTEAL FAUCET OF A **GIANT WOMAN**, TO WHOM THE *ARTHUR* AND HER CREW WERE NO GREATER IN SCALE THAN THE COMMON BOAR WASP, PEACOCK LEECH, OR MUSK APHID!

WHAT A SITUATION!

AND NOW ON WITH OUR STORY...

BY STEVE STILES & DICK LUPOFF

NOW LADS, WE SEEM TO HAVE LANDED IN AN **INOPPORTUNE** LOCALE...

I THINK WE WOULD BE WISE TO, AHEM, *"PULL UP STAKES"* IF I MAY BE PERMITTED A TENSION RELIEVING **WITTICISM.**

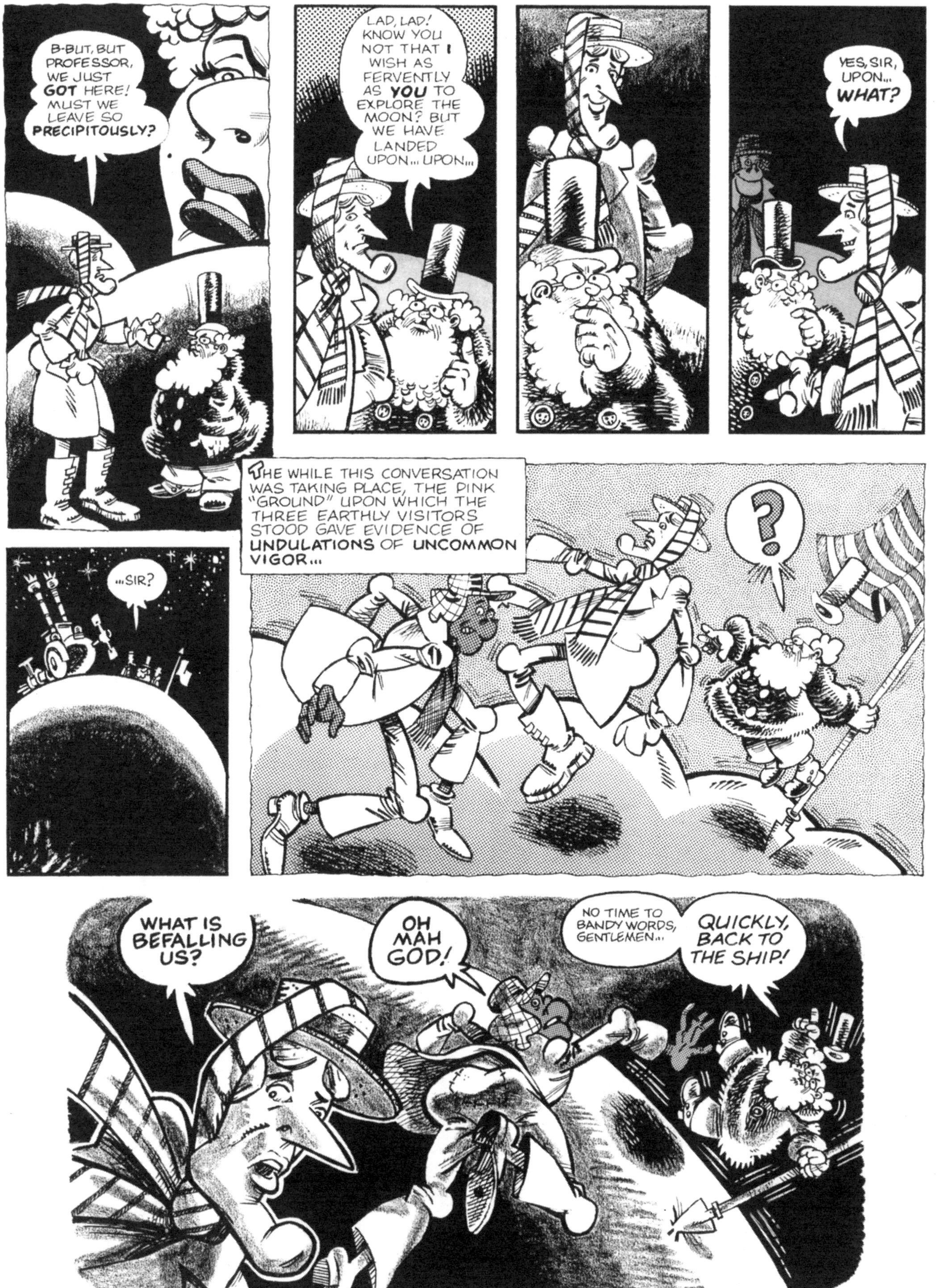
B-BUT, BUT PROFESSOR, WE JUST **GOT** HERE! MUST WE LEAVE SO **PRECIPITOUSLY?**
LAD, LAD! KNOW YOU NOT THAT **I** WISH AS FERVENTLY AS **YOU** TO EXPLORE THE MOON? BUT WE HAVE LANDED UPON... UPON...
YES, SIR, UPON... **WHAT?**
THE WHILE THIS CONVERSATION WAS TAKING PLACE, THE PINK "GROUND" UPON WHICH THE THREE EARTHLY VISITORS STOOD GAVE EVIDENCE OF **UNDULATIONS** OF **UNCOMMON VIGOR**...
...SIR?
?
WHAT IS BEFALLING US?
OH MAH GOD!
NO TIME TO BANDY WORDS, GENTLEMEN...
QUICKLY, BACK TO THE SHIP!

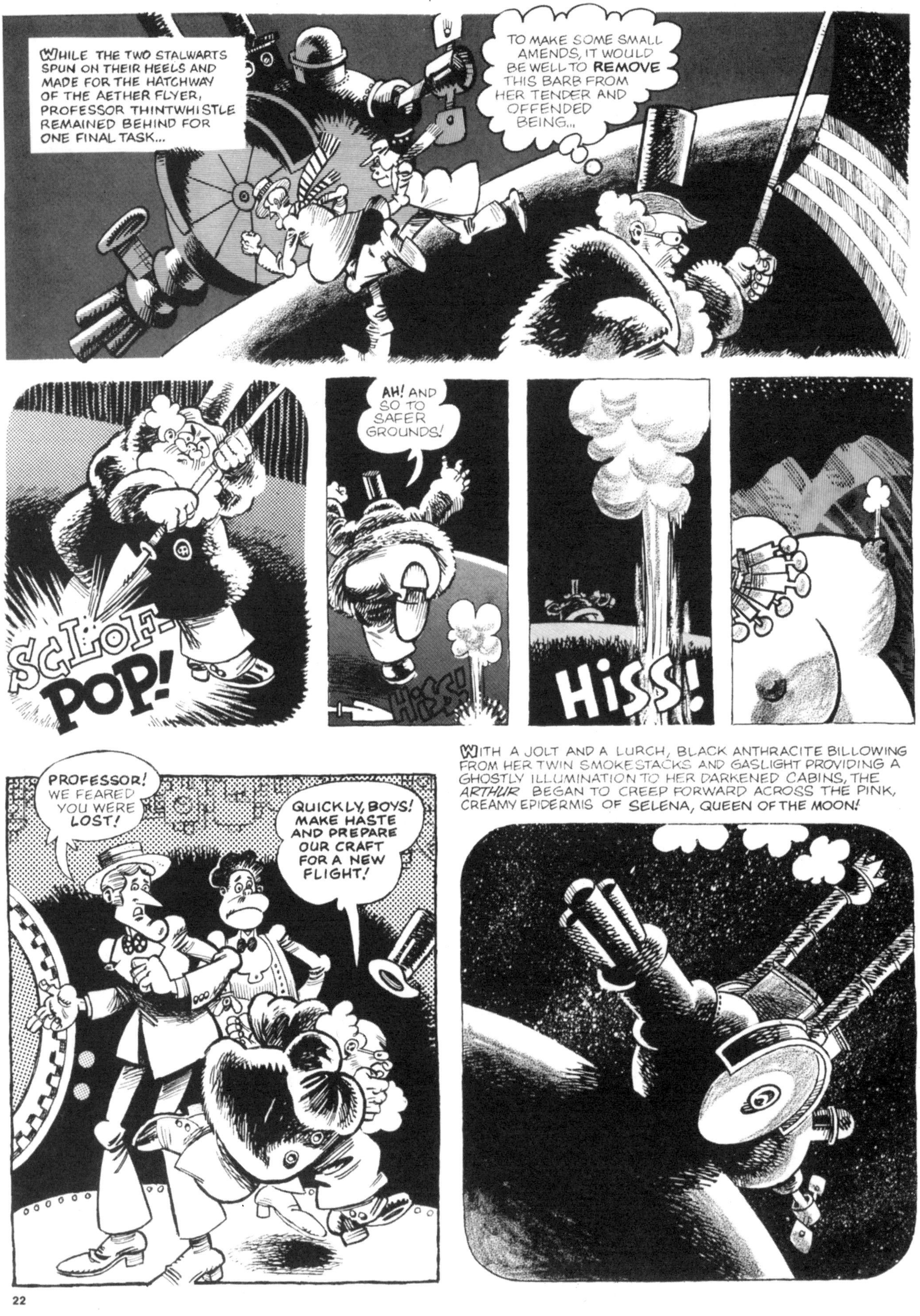

WHILE THE TWO STALWARTS SPUN ON THEIR HEELS AND MADE FOR THE HATCHWAY OF THE AETHER FLYER, PROFESSOR THINTWHISTLE REMAINED BEHIND FOR ONE FINAL TASK...
TO MAKE SOME SMALL AMENDS, IT WOULD BE WELL TO REMOVE THIS BARB FROM HER TENDER AND OFFENDED BEING...
SCLOF-POP!
AH! AND SO TO SAFER GROUNDS!
HISS!
HISS!
PROFESSOR! WE FEARED YOU WERE LOST!
QUICKLY, BOYS! MAKE HASTE AND PREPARE OUR CRAFT FOR A NEW FLIGHT!
WITH A JOLT AND A LURCH, BLACK ANTHRACITE BILLOWING FROM HER TWIN SMOKESTACKS AND GASLIGHT PROVIDING A GHOSTLY ILLUMINATION TO HER DARKENED CABINS, THE *ARTHUR* BEGAN TO CREEP FORWARD ACROSS THE PINK, CREAMY EPIDERMIS OF SELENA, QUEEN OF THE MOON!

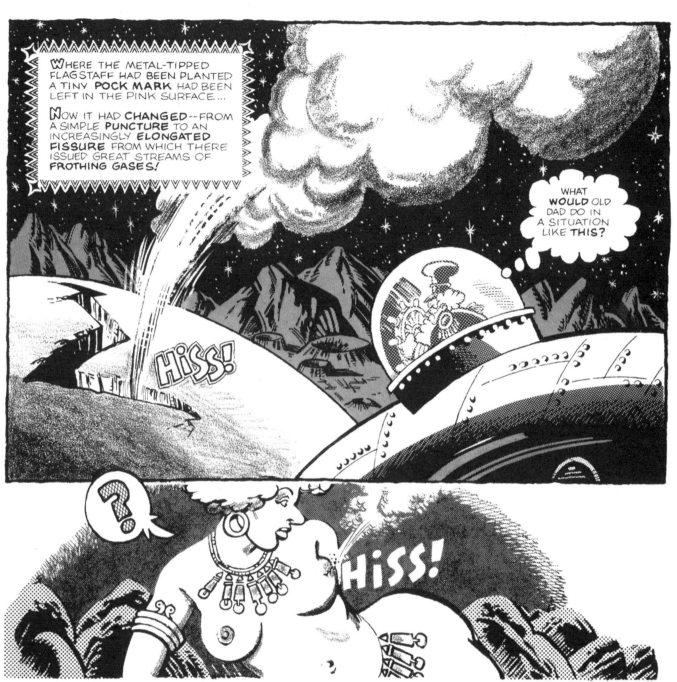

WHERE THE METAL-TIPPED FLAGSTAFF HAD BEEN PLANTED A TINY **POCK MARK** HAD BEEN LEFT IN THE PINK SURFACE...

NOW IT HAD **CHANGED**--FROM A SIMPLE **PUNCTURE** TO AN INCREASINGLY **ELONGATED FISSURE** FROM WHICH THERE ISSUED GREAT STREAMS OF **FROTHING GASES!**

WHAT **WOULD** OLD DAD DO IN A SITUATION LIKE **THIS?**

HISS!

HISS!

WHAT HO!

AHOY THERE IN THE BOILER ROOM! ARE YOU THERE? MORE STEAM, YOU **LAZY BABOON!**

YASSAH!

AH IS GWINE AS FAST'S AH CAN!

WITH A FINAL GLANCE AT THE EVER-ENLARGING FISSURE, THE LEARNED SAGE LIPPED ONE MORE PRAYER AND THREW HIS GEAR LEVER INTO HIGH...

VROOM! VROOM!

AND BARELY IN THE NICK OF TIME, FOR AS THE STURDY SHIP RESPONDED, ANTHRACITE SMOKE BILLOWING FROM HER TWIN SMOKESTACKS, THE GARGANTUAN SELENA DREW HERSELF UP TO A FULLY **UPRIGHT** POSTURE!

SENDING THE HELPLESS CRAFT AND HER CREW SPINNING ACROSS THE QUEEN'S EPIDERMIS, TOWARD THE GLOWING DEPTHS OF THE EVER-ENLARGING **FISSURE!**

HOLD TIGHT, FELLOWS! WE ARE FALLING IN, AND WHAT BETIDES US NOW NONE CAN FORSEE!

SHE-IT!

NOR, INDEED, COULD ANYONE HAVE FORESEEN THE **ASTOUNDING VISION** WHICH AWAITED THE THREE TRAVELERS AS THEIR HARDY CRAFT SHOT INTO THE WIDENING CRACK WHICH HAD OPENED IN THE SHRINKING BREAST ...

GOODNESS GRACIOUS!

NO ARTERIES, BONE, OR MUSCLE TISSUE DID THEY SEE, BUT INSTEAD SOME **WILDLY FEVERED SPECTACLE** BEYOND THE CRAZED IMAGININGS OF THE SORDID **OPIUM ADDICT** A-DREAMING IN HIS SMOKY DEN ...

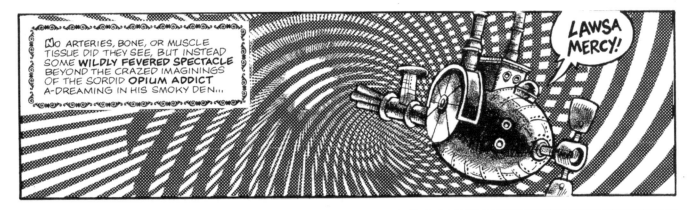

LAWSA MERCY!

AS THE *ARTHUR* HURTLED FORWARD AT THE UNHEARD OF VELOCITY OF **650 MILES PER HOUR** TRANSCENDING THE VERY **NATURAL PHILOSOPHIES** IN ITS SPEED UNTIL THE **UNIVERSAL ESSENCE** OF **TIME** AND **SPACE** WAS UTTERLY **CONFOUNDED!**

IS THERE YET HOPE?

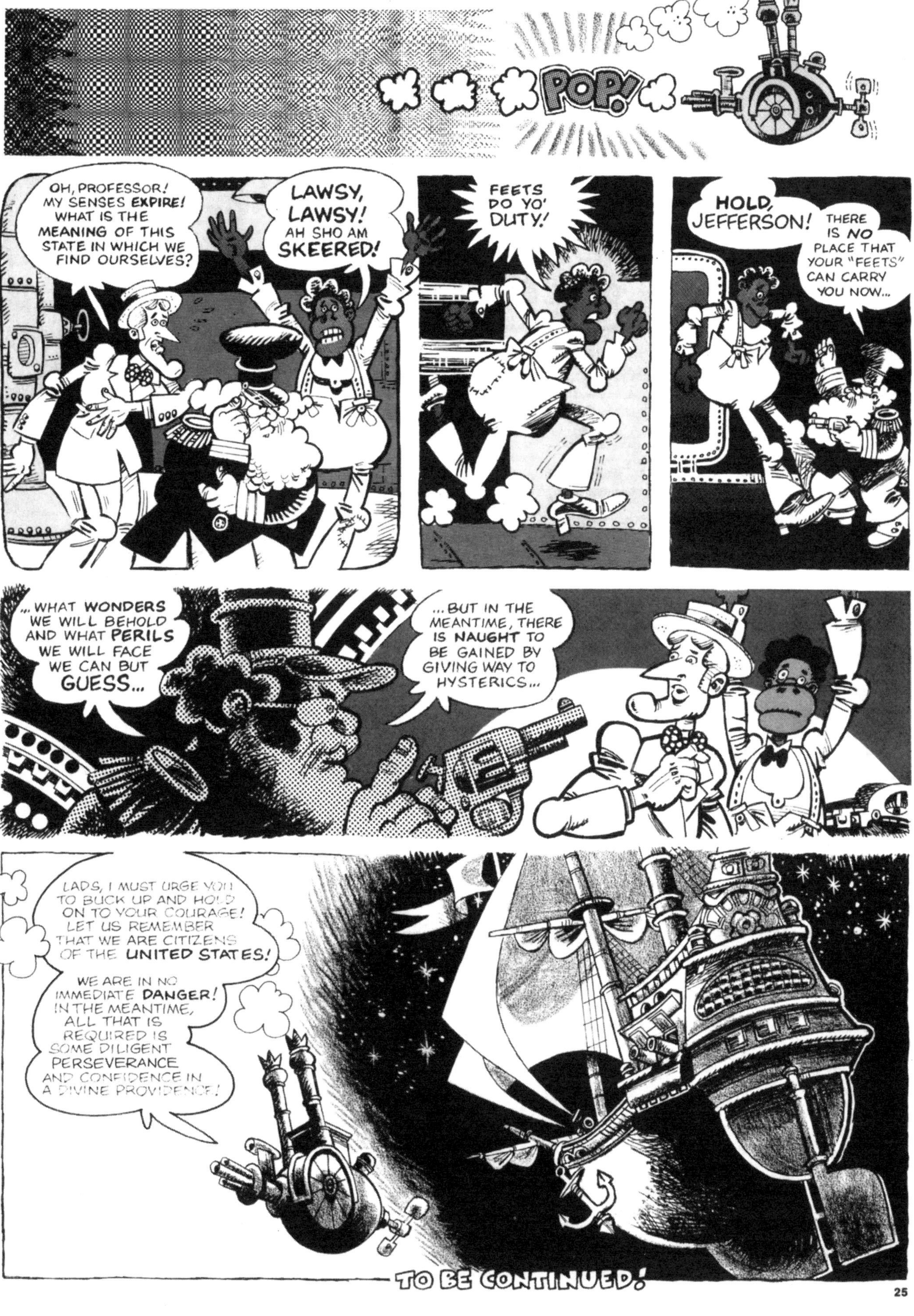
POP!
OH, PROFESSOR! MY SENSES EXPIRE! WHAT IS THE MEANING OF THIS STATE IN WHICH WE FIND OURSELVES?
LAWSY, LAWSY! AH SHO AM SKEERED!
FEETS DO YO' DUTY!
HOLD, JEFFERSON!
THERE IS NO PLACE THAT YOUR "FEETS" CAN CARRY YOU NOW...
...WHAT WONDERS WE WILL BEHOLD AND WHAT PERILS WE WILL FACE WE CAN BUT GUESS...
...BUT IN THE MEANTIME, THERE IS NAUGHT TO BE GAINED BY GIVING WAY TO HYSTERICS...
LADS, I MUST URGE YOU TO BUCK UP AND HOLD ON TO YOUR COURAGE! LET US REMEMBER THAT WE ARE CITIZENS OF THE UNITED STATES!
WE ARE IN NO IMMEDIATE DANGER! IN THE MEANTIME, ALL THAT IS REQUIRED IS SOME DILIGENT PERSEVERANCE AND CONFIDENCE IN A DIVINE PROVIDENCE!
TO BE CONTINUED!

THE ADVENTURES OF PROFESSOR THINTWHISTLE AND HIS INCREDIBLE AETHER FLYER

CHAPTER FIVE: WELL, DEAR READER, TO RECOUNT THE PREVIOUS UNPRECEDENTED EXPERIENCES OF SCIENTIFIC WONDER WOULD BE A DISSERTATION *CHOKED* WITH INTEREST, BUT TO COMPRESS THIS MAGNITUDE INTO A **NUTSHELL**, LET ME ONLY SAY THAT THE *CHESTER ALAN ARTHUR* (AN INGENIOUS "**STEAM POWER**" VESSEL, LATE OF BUFFALO FALLS, PA.) HAD PASSED BEYOND MERELY **FLYING** AND HAD ADVANCED SO FAR AS TO JOURNEY TO THE **MOON!** HOWEVER, MORE IMPROPERLY, THE BULK OF THE *ARTHUR* RESTED UPON A **VAST MILK-SECRETING ORGAN** FOUND UPON THE BREAST OF CERTAIN MEMBERS OF OUR SPECIES; IN SHORT, A **BOSOM!** SPECULATION MUST WAIT, FOR AFTER THE ACCIDENTAL PUNCTURING OF THIS **ORGAN** THE *ARTHUR*, WITH ALL HANDS, TUMBLED WITHIN-- FINDING NOT **MILK**, BUT, RATHER, A MIND-CONFOUNDING **VISTA!** RATHER THAN FURTHER STRUGGLE WITH SUCH A COMPLICATED BURDEN OF EXPOSITION, LET US NOW ***PROCEED.*** **ON WITH THE STORY!**

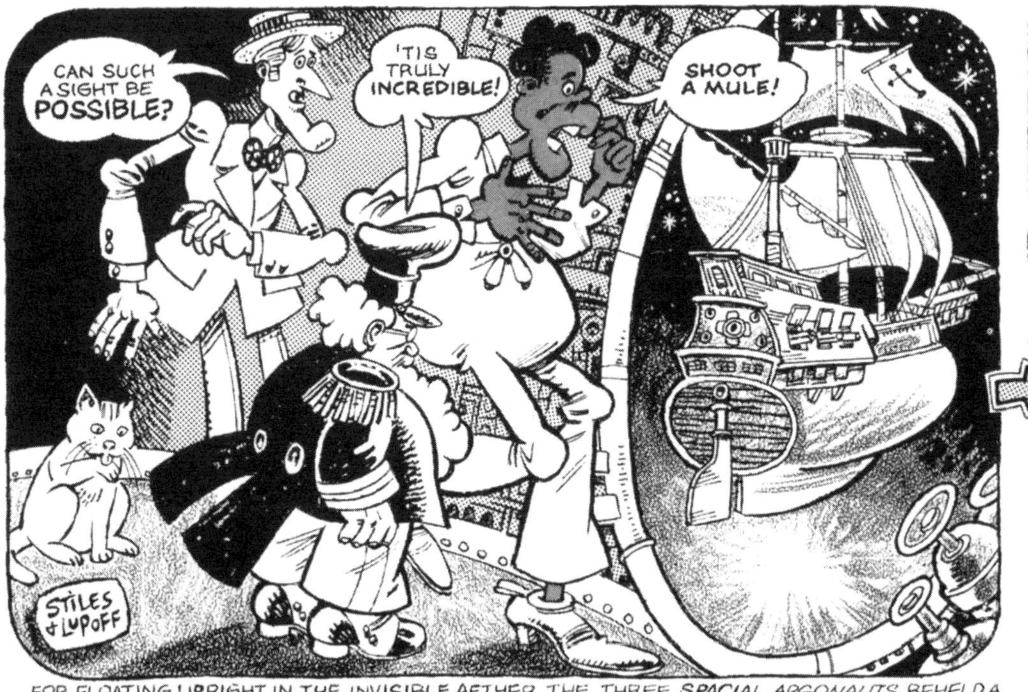

CAN SUCH A SIGHT BE POSSIBLE?
'TIS TRULY INCREDIBLE!
SHOOT A MULE!
STILES & LUPOFF

...FOR FLOATING UPRIGHT IN THE INVISIBLE AETHER THE THREE *SPACIAL ARGONAUTS* BEHELD A SPLENDID **SPANISH GALLEON** FROM A PREVIOUS CENTURY REMOVED FROM THE NINETEENTH!

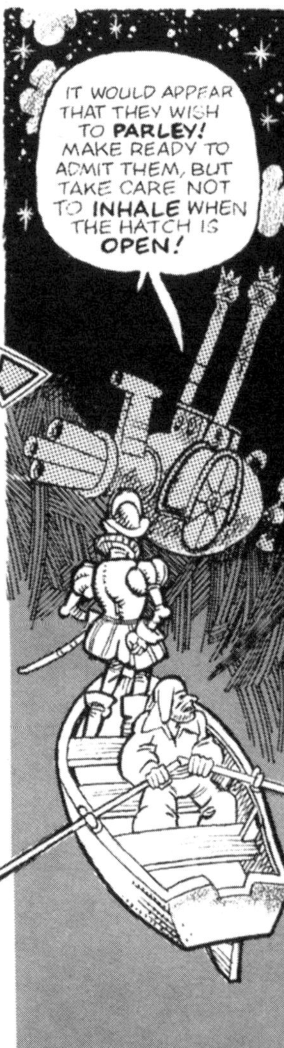

IT WOULD APPEAR THAT THEY WISH TO PARLEY! MAKE READY TO ADMIT THEM, BUT TAKE CARE NOT TO INHALE WHEN THE HATCH IS OPEN!

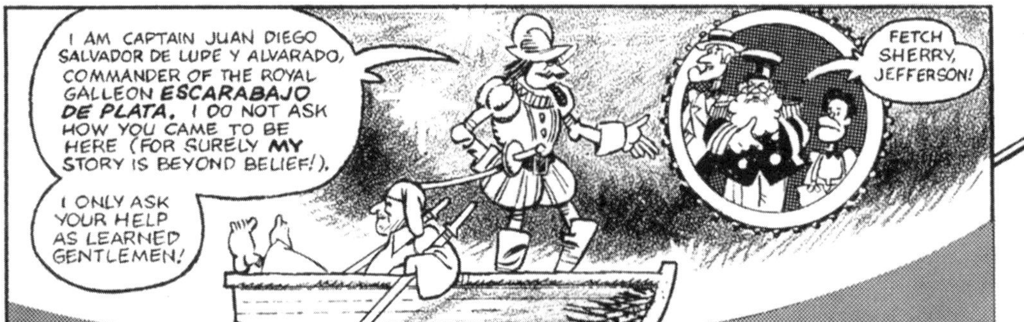

I AM CAPTAIN JUAN DIEGO SALVADOR DE LUPE Y ALVARADO, COMMANDER OF THE ROYAL GALLEON ESCARABAJO DE PLATA. I DO NOT ASK HOW YOU CAME TO BE HERE (FOR SURELY MY STORY IS BEYOND BELIEF!).
I ONLY ASK YOUR HELP AS LEARNED GENTLEMEN!
FETCH SHERRY, JEFFERSON!

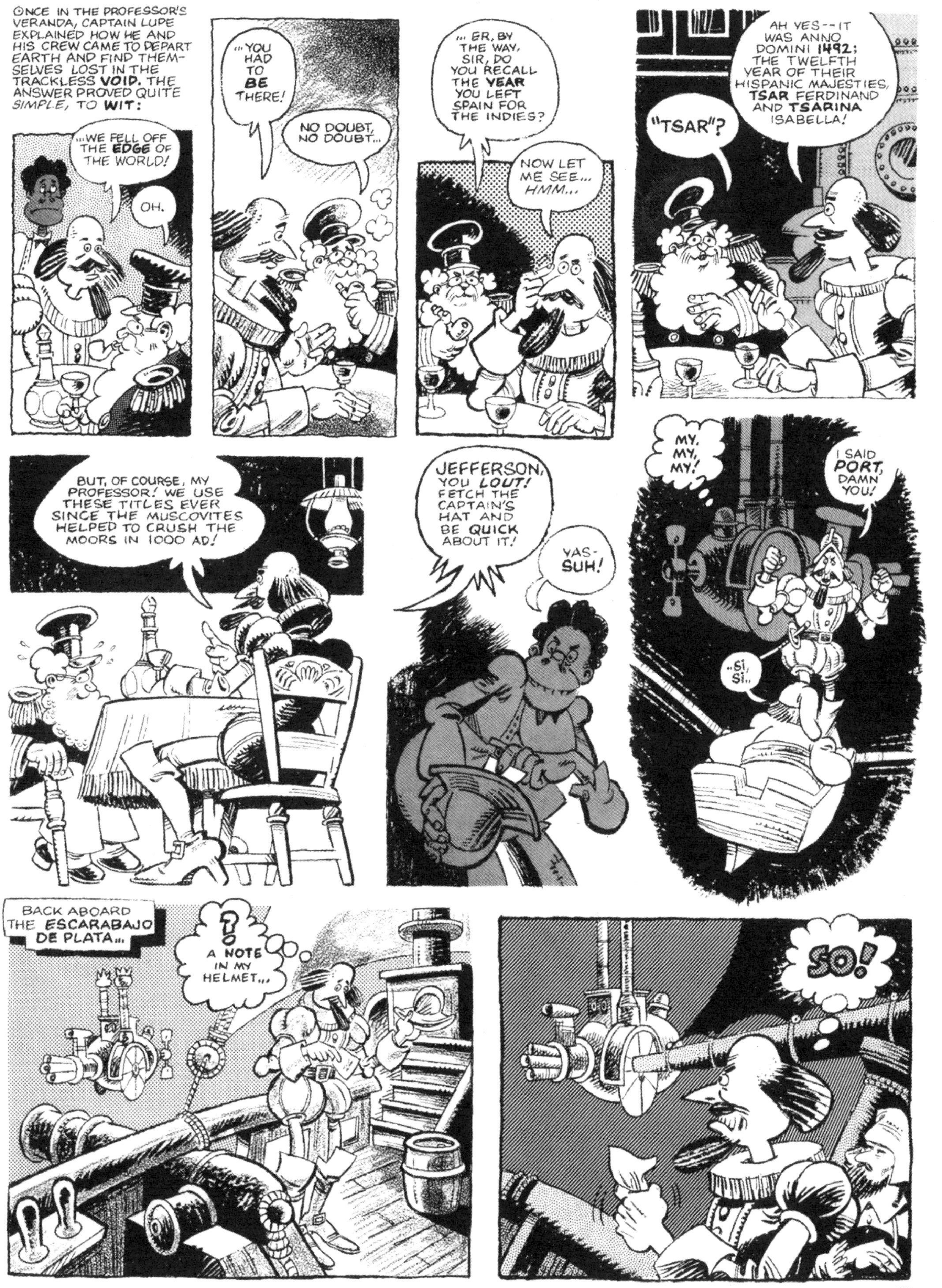
ONCE IN THE PROFESSOR'S VERANDA, CAPTAIN LUPE EXPLAINED HOW HE AND HIS CREW CAME TO DEPART EARTH AND FIND THEMSELVES LOST IN THE TRACKLESS VOID. THE ANSWER PROVED QUITE SIMPLE, TO WIT:
...WE FELL OFF THE EDGE OF THE WORLD!
OH.
...YOU HAD TO BE THERE!
NO DOUBT, NO DOUBT...
... ER, BY THE WAY, SIR, DO YOU RECALL THE YEAR YOU LEFT SPAIN FOR THE INDIES?
NOW LET ME SEE... HMM...
AH YES--IT WAS ANNO DOMINI 1492: THE TWELFTH YEAR OF THEIR HISPANIC MAJESTIES, TSAR FERDINAND AND TSARINA ISABELLA!
"TSAR"?
BUT, OF COURSE, MY PROFESSOR! WE USE THESE TITLES EVER SINCE THE MUSCOVITES HELPED TO CRUSH THE MOORS IN 1000 AD!
JEFFERSON, YOU LOUT! FETCH THE CAPTAIN'S HAT AND BE QUICK ABOUT IT!
YAS-SUH!
MY, MY, MY!
I SAID PORT, DAMN YOU!
..SI, SI..
BACK ABOARD THE ESCARABAJO DE PLATA...
?
A NOTE IN MY HELMET...
SO!

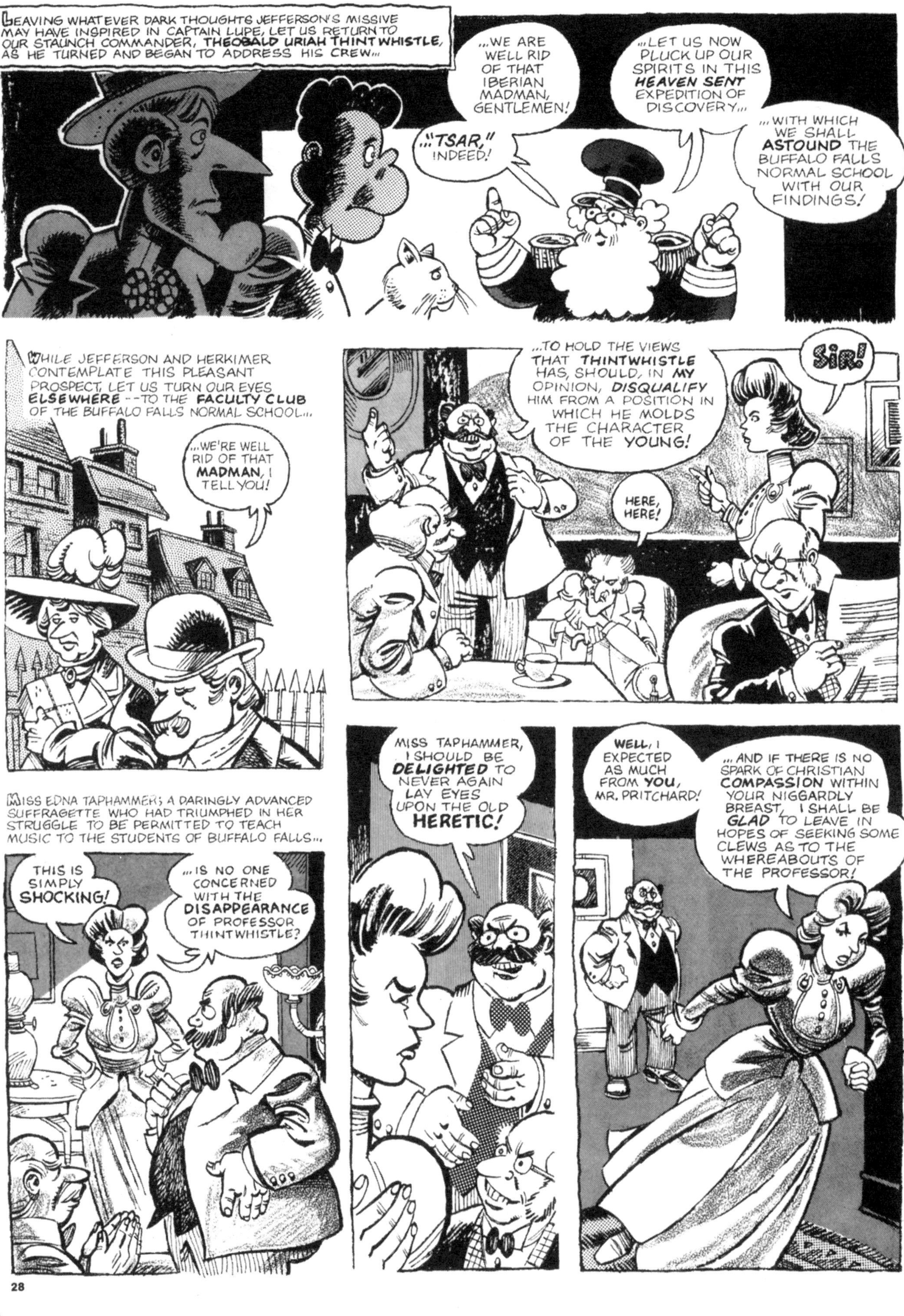
LEAVING WHATEVER DARK THOUGHTS JEFFERSON'S MISSIVE MAY HAVE INSPIRED IN CAPTAIN LUPE, LET US RETURN TO OUR STAUNCH COMMANDER, THEOBALD URIAH THINTWHISTLE, AS HE TURNED AND BEGAN TO ADDRESS HIS CREW...
...WE ARE WELL RID OF THAT IBERIAN MADMAN, GENTLEMEN!
..."TSAR," INDEED!
...LET US NOW PLUCK UP OUR SPIRITS IN THIS HEAVEN SENT EXPEDITION OF DISCOVERY...
...WITH WHICH WE SHALL ASTOUND THE BUFFALO FALLS NORMAL SCHOOL WITH OUR FINDINGS!
WHILE JEFFERSON AND HERKIMER CONTEMPLATE THIS PLEASANT PROSPECT, LET US TURN OUR EYES ELSEWHERE --TO THE FACULTY CLUB OF THE BUFFALO FALLS NORMAL SCHOOL...
...WE'RE WELL RID OF THAT MADMAN, I TELL YOU!
...TO HOLD THE VIEWS THAT THINTWHISTLE HAS, SHOULD, IN MY OPINION, DISQUALIFY HIM FROM A POSITION IN WHICH HE MOLDS THE CHARACTER OF THE YOUNG!
HERE, HERE!
SIR!
MISS EDNA TAPHAMMER, A DARINGLY ADVANCED SUFFRAGETTE WHO HAD TRIUMPHED IN HER STRUGGLE TO BE PERMITTED TO TEACH MUSIC TO THE STUDENTS OF BUFFALO FALLS...
THIS IS SIMPLY SHOCKING!
...IS NO ONE CONCERNED WITH THE DISAPPEARANCE OF PROFESSOR THINTWHISTLE?
MISS TAPHAMMER, I SHOULD BE DELIGHTED TO NEVER AGAIN LAY EYES UPON THE OLD HERETIC!
WELL, I EXPECTED AS MUCH FROM YOU, MR. PRITCHARD!
...AND IF THERE IS NO SPARK OF CHRISTIAN COMPASSION WITHIN YOUR NIGGARDLY BREAST, I SHALL BE GLAD TO LEAVE IN HOPES OF SEEKING SOME CLEWS AS TO THE WHEREABOUTS OF THE PROFESSOR!

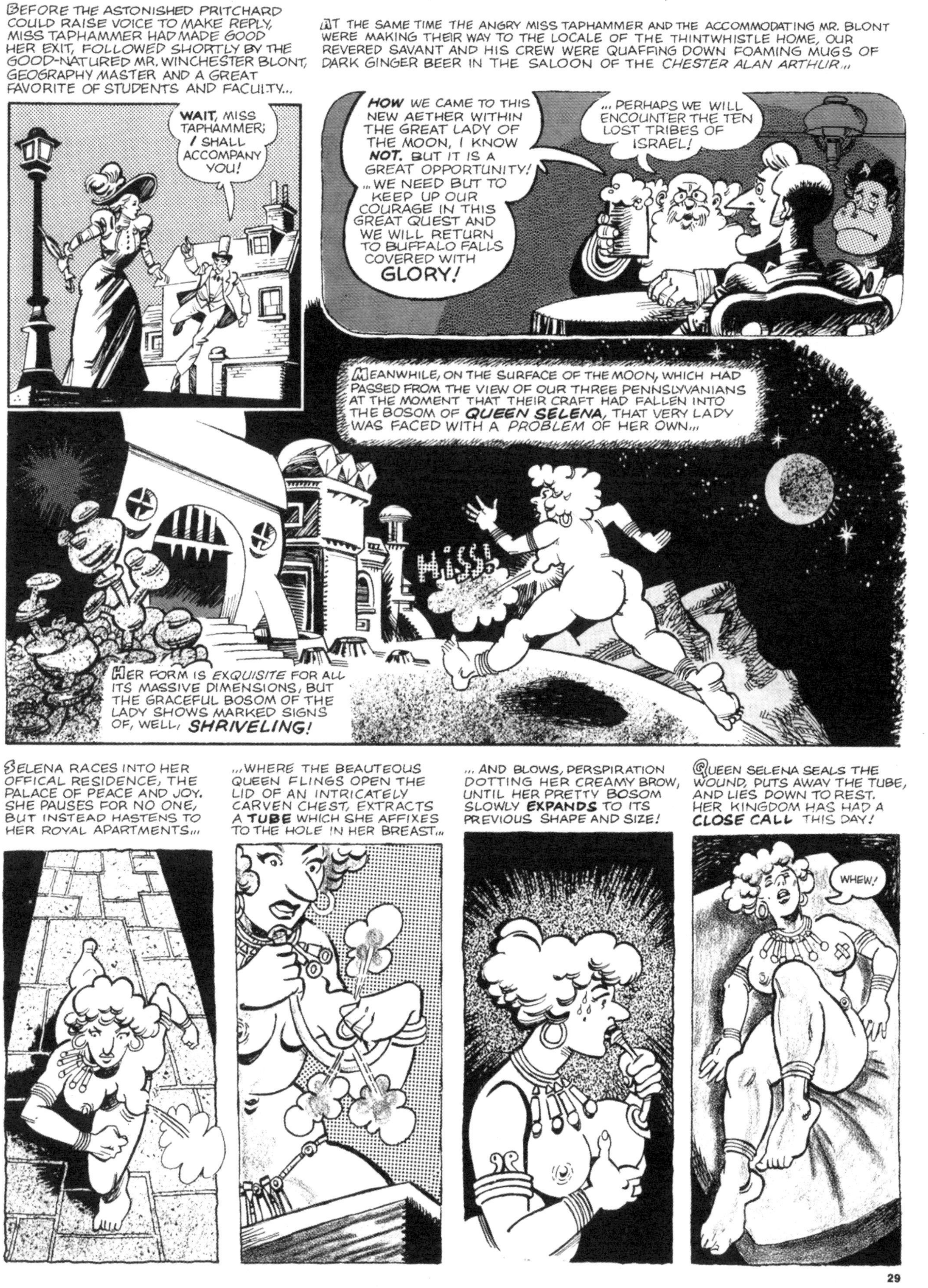
BEFORE THE ASTONISHED PRITCHARD COULD RAISE VOICE TO MAKE REPLY, MISS TAPHAMMER HAD MADE GOOD HER EXIT, FOLLOWED SHORTLY BY THE GOOD-NATURED MR. WINCHESTER BLONT, GEOGRAPHY MASTER AND A GREAT FAVORITE OF STUDENTS AND FACULTY...
WAIT, MISS TAPHAMMER; I SHALL ACCOMPANY YOU!
AT THE SAME TIME THE ANGRY MISS TAPHAMMER AND THE ACCOMMODATING MR. BLONT WERE MAKING THEIR WAY TO THE LOCALE OF THE THINTWHISTLE HOME, OUR REVERED SAVANT AND HIS CREW WERE QUAFFING DOWN FOAMING MUGS OF DARK GINGER BEER IN THE SALOON OF THE CHESTER ALAN ARTHUR...
HOW WE CAME TO THIS NEW AETHER WITHIN THE GREAT LADY OF THE MOON, I KNOW NOT. BUT IT IS A GREAT OPPORTUNITY! ...WE NEED BUT TO KEEP UP OUR COURAGE IN THIS GREAT QUEST AND WE WILL RETURN TO BUFFALO FALLS COVERED WITH GLORY!
...PERHAPS WE WILL ENCOUNTER THE TEN LOST TRIBES OF ISRAEL!
MEANWHILE, ON THE SURFACE OF THE MOON, WHICH HAD PASSED FROM THE VIEW OF OUR THREE PENNSLYVANIANS AT THE MOMENT THAT THEIR CRAFT HAD FALLEN INTO THE BOSOM OF QUEEN SELENA, THAT VERY LADY WAS FACED WITH A PROBLEM OF HER OWN...
HISS
HER FORM IS EXQUISITE FOR ALL ITS MASSIVE DIMENSIONS, BUT THE GRACEFUL BOSOM OF THE LADY SHOWS MARKED SIGNS OF, WELL, SHRIVELING!
SELENA RACES INTO HER OFFICAL RESIDENCE, THE PALACE OF PEACE AND JOY. SHE PAUSES FOR NO ONE, BUT INSTEAD HASTENS TO HER ROYAL APARTMENTS...
...WHERE THE BEAUTEOUS QUEEN FLINGS OPEN THE LID OF AN INTRICATELY CARVEN CHEST, EXTRACTS A TUBE WHICH SHE AFFIXES TO THE HOLE IN HER BREAST...
...AND BLOWS, PERSPIRATION DOTTING HER CREAMY BROW, UNTIL HER PRETTY BOSOM SLOWLY EXPANDS TO ITS PREVIOUS SHAPE AND SIZE!
QUEEN SELENA SEALS THE WOUND, PUTS AWAY THE TUBE, AND LIES DOWN TO REST. HER KINGDOM HAS HAD A CLOSE CALL THIS DAY!
WHEW!

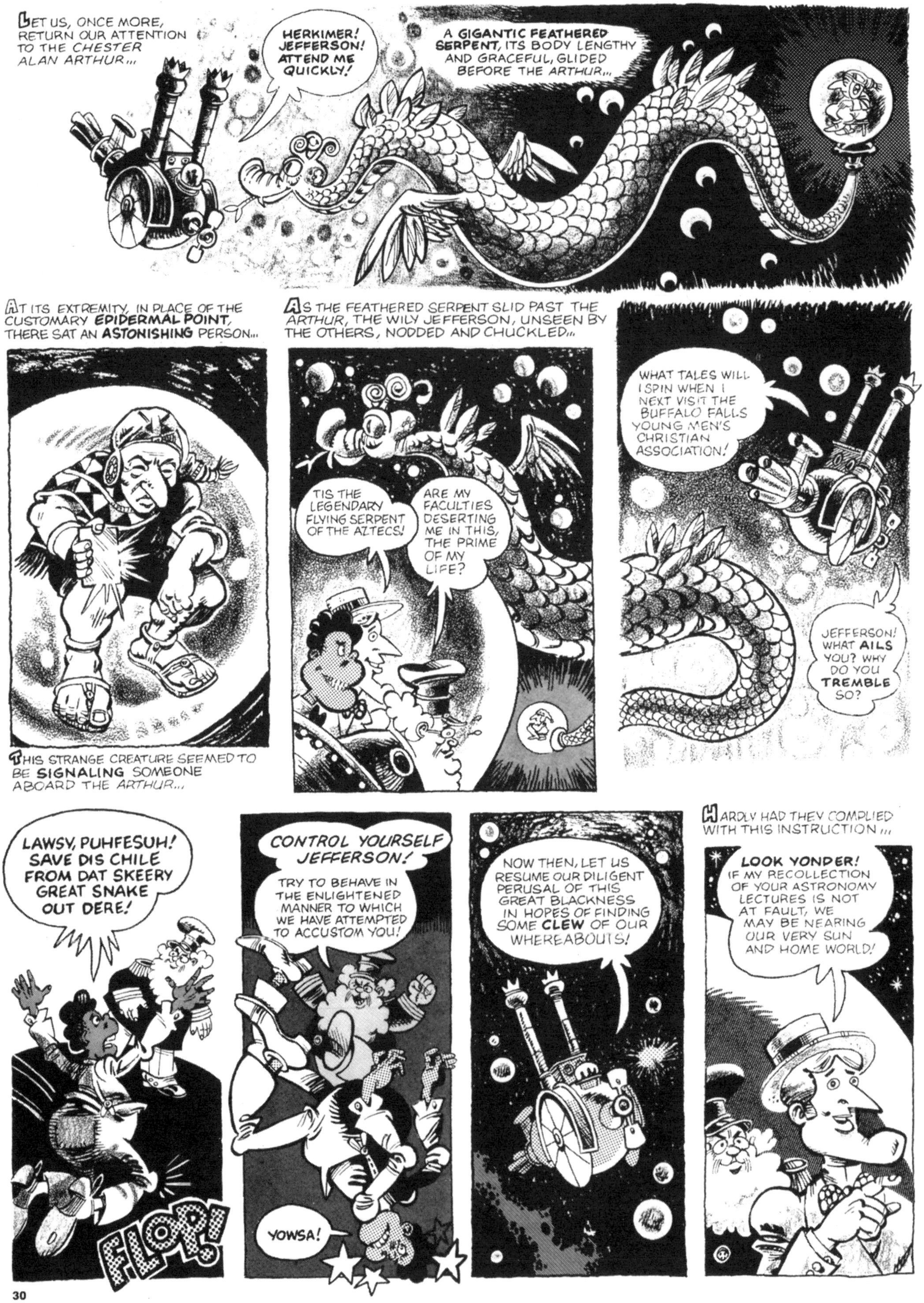
LET US, ONCE MORE, RETURN OUR ATTENTION TO THE CHESTER ALAN ARTHUR...
HERKIMER! JEFFERSON! ATTEND ME QUICKLY!
A GIGANTIC FEATHERED SERPENT, ITS BODY LENGTHY AND GRACEFUL, GLIDED BEFORE THE ARTHUR...
AT ITS EXTREMITY, IN PLACE OF THE CUSTOMARY EPIDERMAL POINT, THERE SAT AN ASTONISHING PERSON...
THIS STRANGE CREATURE SEEMED TO BE SIGNALING SOMEONE ABOARD THE ARTHUR...
AS THE FEATHERED SERPENT SLID PAST THE ARTHUR, THE WILY JEFFERSON, UNSEEN BY THE OTHERS, NODDED AND CHUCKLED...
TIS THE LEGENDARY FLYING SERPENT OF THE AZTECS!
ARE MY FACULTIES DESERTING ME IN THIS, THE PRIME OF MY LIFE?
WHAT TALES WILL I SPIN WHEN I NEXT VISIT THE BUFFALO FALLS YOUNG MEN'S CHRISTIAN ASSOCIATION!
JEFFERSON! WHAT AILS YOU? WHY DO YOU TREMBLE SO?
LAWSY, PUHFESUH! SAVE DIS CHILE FROM DAT SKEERY GREAT SNAKE OUT DERE!
FLOP!
CONTROL YOURSELF JEFFERSON!
TRY TO BEHAVE IN THE ENLIGHTENED MANNER TO WHICH WE HAVE ATTEMPTED TO ACCUSTOM YOU!
YOWSA!
NOW THEN, LET US RESUME OUR DILIGENT PERUSAL OF THIS GREAT BLACKNESS IN HOPES OF FINDING SOME CLEW OF OUR WHEREABOUTS!
HARDLY HAD THEY COMPLIED WITH THIS INSTRUCTION...
LOOK YONDER! IF MY RECOLLECTION OF YOUR ASTRONOMY LECTURES IS NOT AT FAULT, WE MAY BE NEARING OUR VERY SUN AND HOME WORLD!

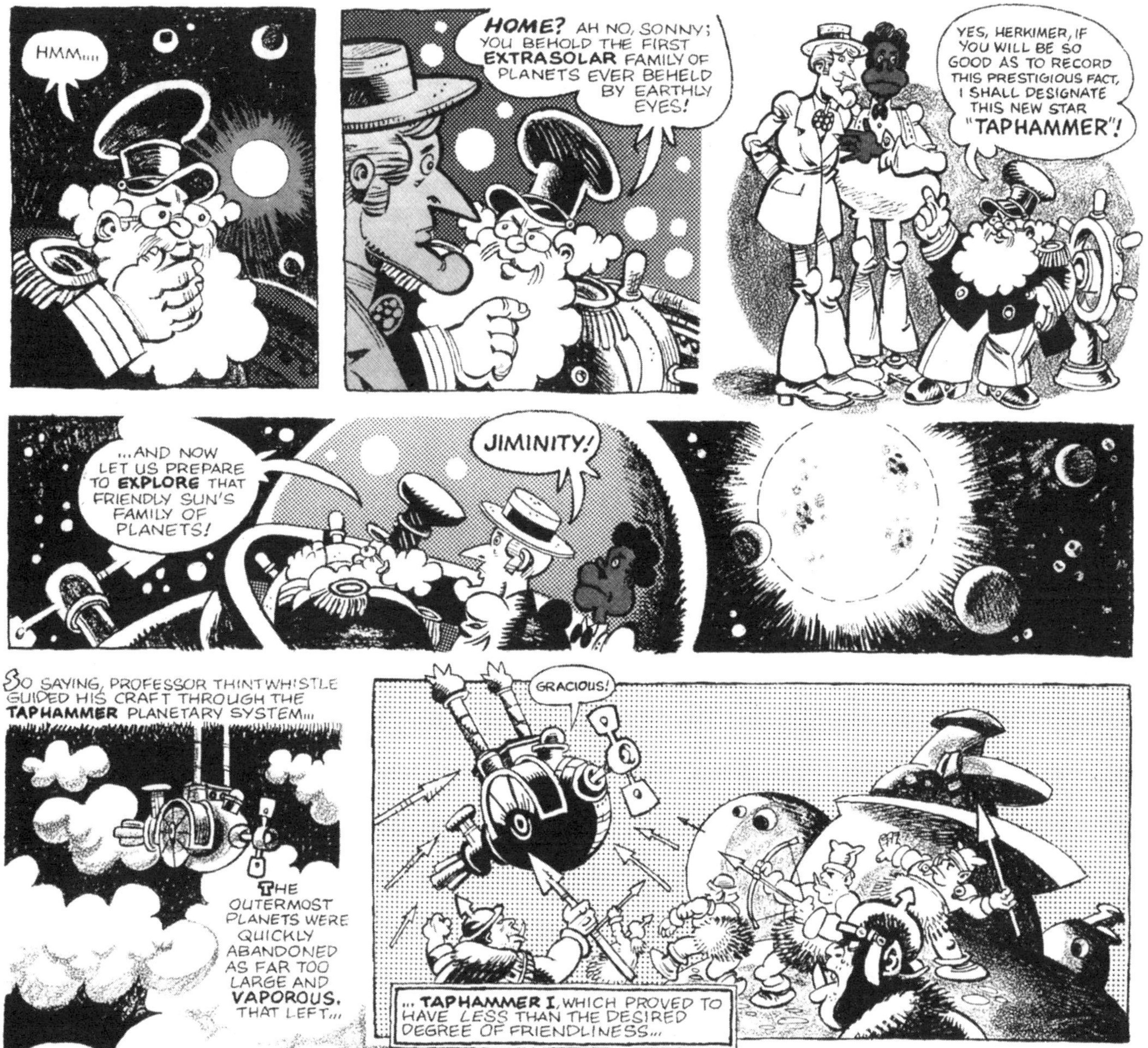

HMM....
HOME? AH NO, SONNY; YOU BEHOLD THE FIRST EXTRASOLAR FAMILY OF PLANETS EVER BEHELD BY EARTHLY EYES!
YES, HERKIMER, IF YOU WILL BE SO GOOD AS TO RECORD THIS PRESTIGIOUS FACT, I SHALL DESIGNATE THIS NEW STAR "TAPHAMMER"!
...AND NOW LET US PREPARE TO EXPLORE THAT FRIENDLY SUN'S FAMILY OF PLANETS!
JIMINITY!
SO SAYING, PROFESSOR THINTWHISTLE GUIDED HIS CRAFT THROUGH THE TAPHAMMER PLANETARY SYSTEM...
THE OUTERMOST PLANETS WERE QUICKLY ABANDONED AS FAR TOO LARGE AND VAPOROUS. THAT LEFT...
GRACIOUS!
... TAPHAMMER I, WHICH PROVED TO HAVE LESS THAN THE DESIRED DEGREE OF FRIENDLINESS...

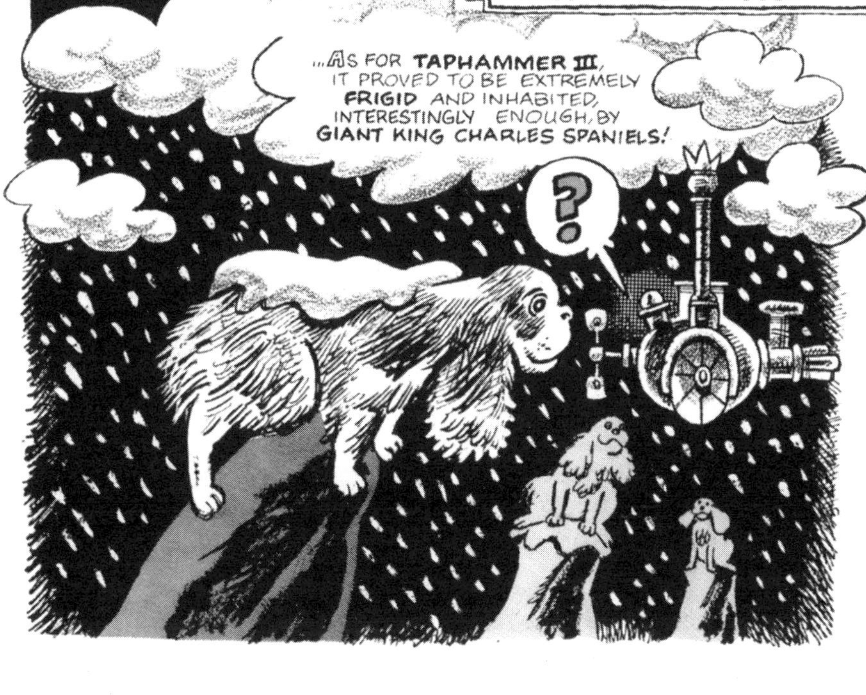

...AS FOR TAPHAMMER III, IT PROVED TO BE EXTREMELY FRIGID AND INHABITED, INTERESTINGLY ENOUGH, BY GIANT KING CHARLES SPANIELS!
?

From the Cabin Boy's Log, May 6, 1884

The expedition of the Aether-flyer continues to blunder from one near disaster to another as incompetent honky pilot **T** and supercargo ofay nincompoop **H** perform as usual; i.e., idiotically.

The Chester Alan Arthur is wandering aimlessly within the "Taphammer" system while communication has been established with Captain Lupe.

Venceremos!

Clay
Cabin Boy

TO BE CONTINUED...

THE ADVENTURES OF PROFESSOR THINTWHISTLE AND HIS INCREDIBLE AETHER FLYER

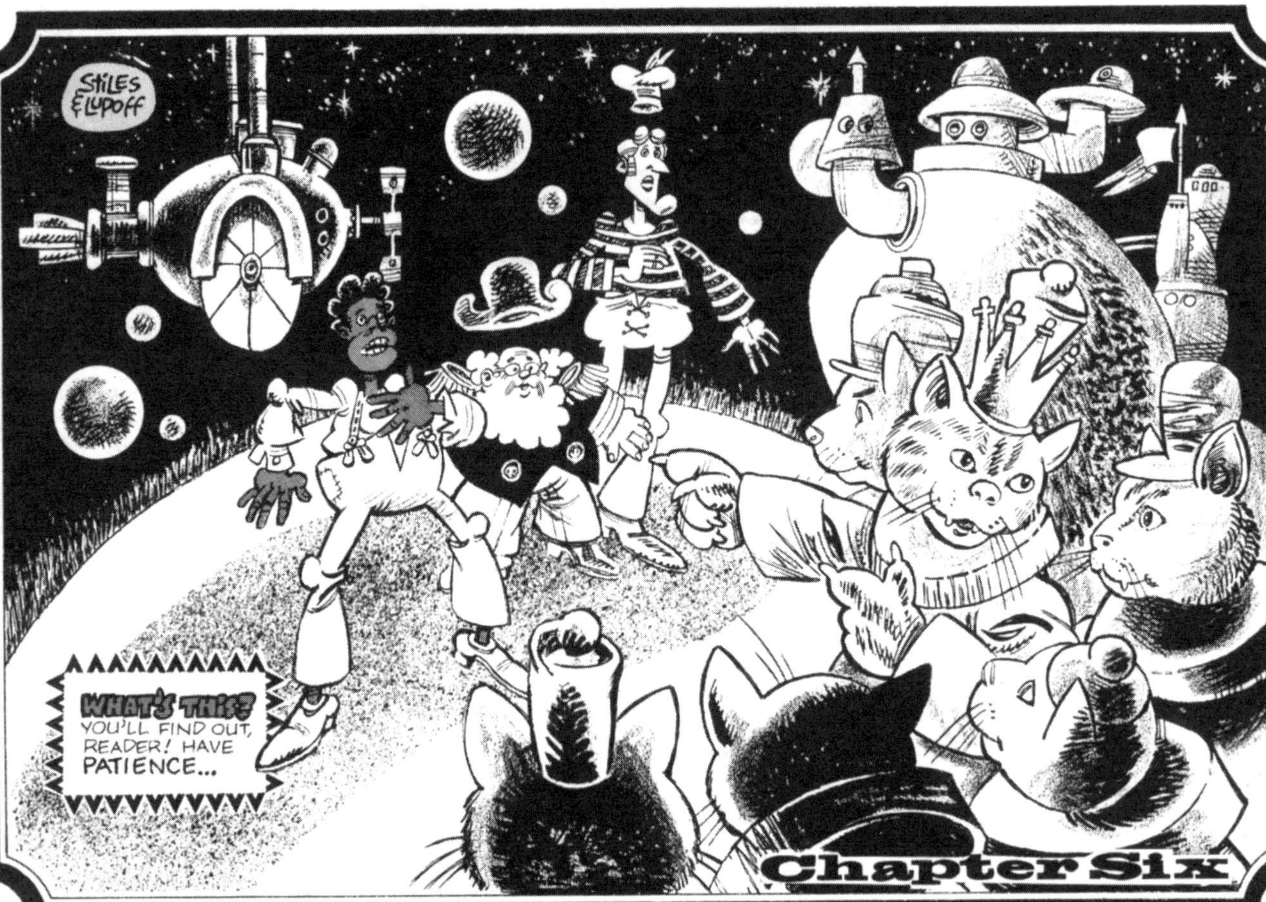
STILES & LUPOFF
WHAT'S THIS? YOU'LL FIND OUT, READER! HAVE PATIENCE...
Chapter Six

...ALL THAT CAN **WAIT!** LET US NOW TURN OUR GAZE TO THE TOWN OF BUFFALO FALLS...

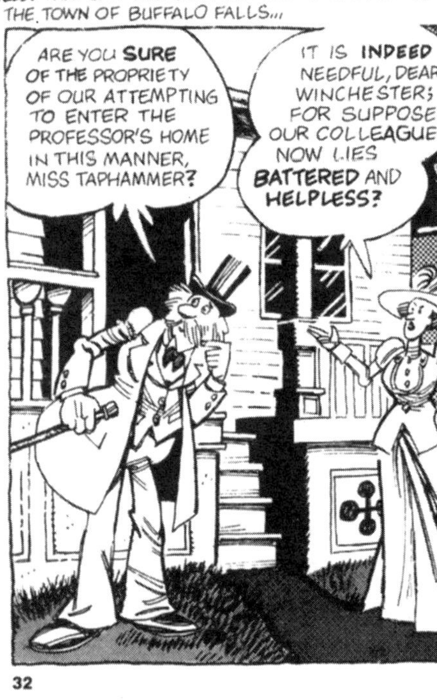
ARE YOU **SURE** OF THE PROPRIETY OF OUR ATTEMPTING TO ENTER THE PROFESSOR'S HOME IN THIS MANNER, MISS TAPHAMMER?
IT IS **INDEED** NEEDFUL, DEAR WINCHESTER; FOR SUPPOSE OUR COLLEAGUE NOW LIES **BATTERED** AND **HELPLESS?**

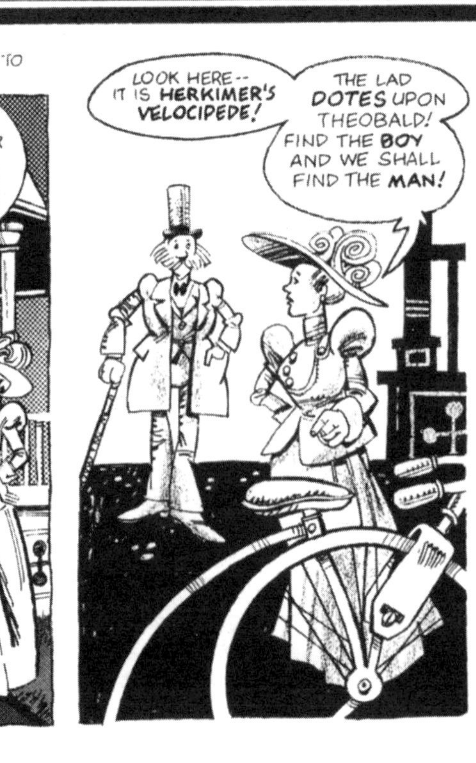
LOOK HERE-- IT IS **HERKIMER'S VELOCIPEDE!**
THE LAD **DOTES** UPON THEOBALD! FIND THE **BOY** AND WE SHALL FIND THE **MAN!**

MR. BLONT TREMULOUSLY ADVANCED INTO THE YARD AND, ESPYING THE SMALL **ANTHRACITE** DIGGING WHICH PROFESSOR THINTWHISTLE HAD INITIATED, RAN TO ITS EDGE...

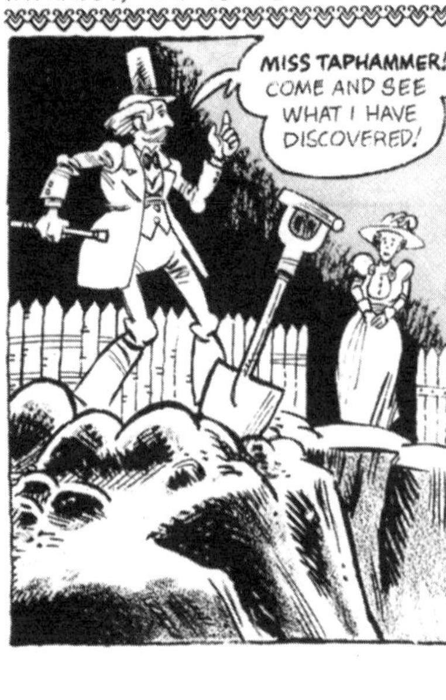
MISS TAPHAMMER! COME AND SEE WHAT I HAVE DISCOVERED!

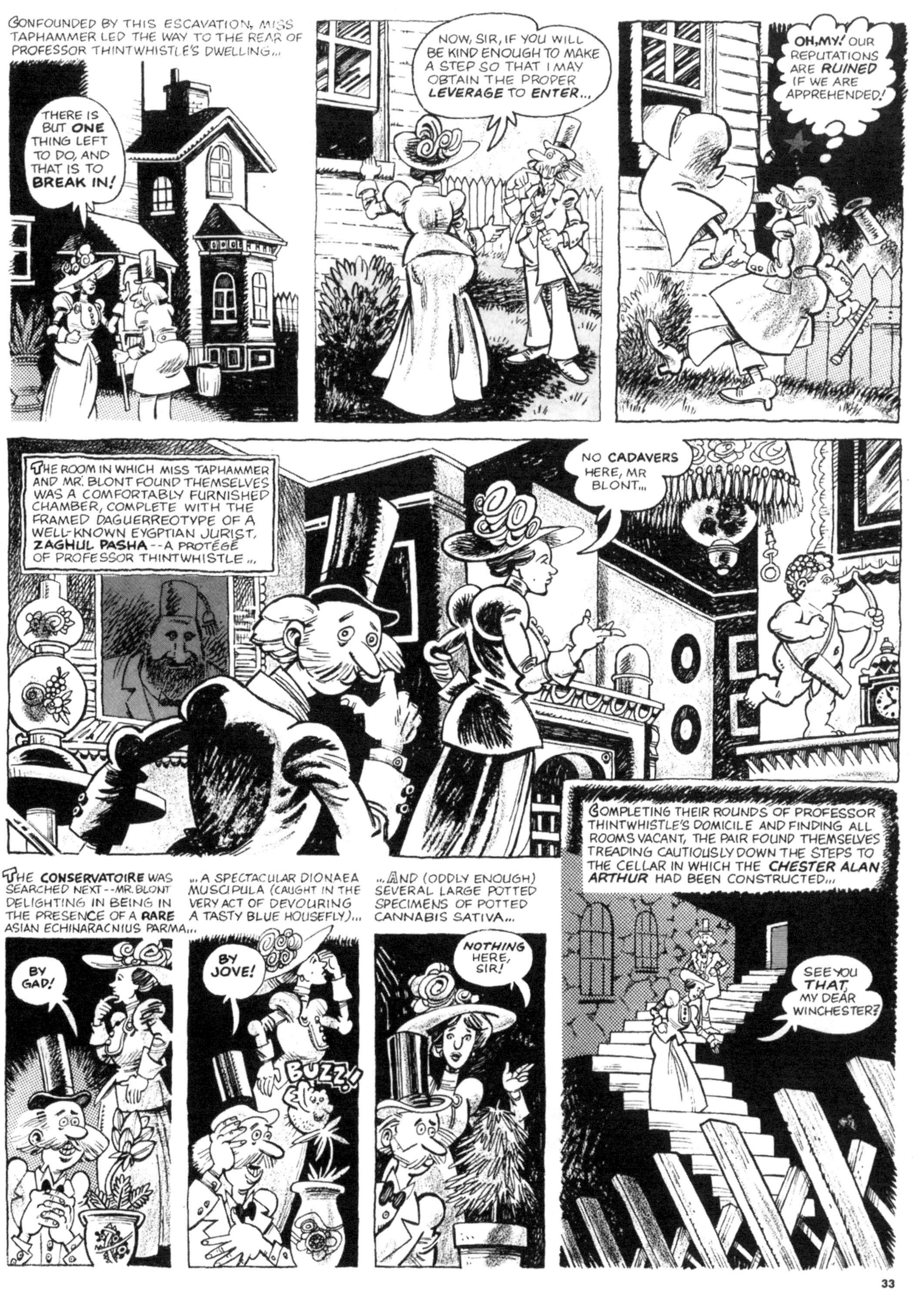

CONFOUNDED BY THIS ESCAVATION, MISS TAPHAMMER LED THE WAY TO THE REAR OF PROFESSOR THINTWHISTLE'S DWELLING...
THERE IS BUT ONE THING LEFT TO DO, AND THAT IS TO BREAK IN!
NOW, SIR, IF YOU WILL BE KIND ENOUGH TO MAKE A STEP SO THAT I MAY OBTAIN THE PROPER LEVERAGE TO ENTER...
OH, MY! OUR REPUTATIONS ARE RUINED IF WE ARE APPREHENDED!
THE ROOM IN WHICH MISS TAPHAMMER AND MR. BLONT FOUND THEMSELVES WAS A COMFORTABLY FURNISHED CHAMBER, COMPLETE WITH THE FRAMED DAGUERREOTYPE OF A WELL-KNOWN EYGPTIAN JURIST, ZAGHUL PASHA--A PROTÉGÉ OF PROFESSOR THINTWHISTLE...
NO CADAVERS HERE, MR BLONT...
THE CONSERVATOIRE WAS SEARCHED NEXT--MR. BLONT DELIGHTING IN BEING IN THE PRESENCE OF A RARE ASIAN ECHINARACNIUS PARMA...
BY GAD!
...A SPECTACULAR DIONAEA MUSCIPULA (CAUGHT IN THE VERY ACT OF DEVOURING A TASTY BLUE HOUSEFLY)...
BY JOVE!
BUZZ!
...AND (ODDLY ENOUGH) SEVERAL LARGE POTTED SPECIMENS OF POTTED CANNABIS SATIVA...
NOTHING HERE, SIR!
COMPLETING THEIR ROUNDS OF PROFESSOR THINTWHISTLE'S DOMICILE AND FINDING ALL ROOMS VACANT, THE PAIR FOUND THEMSELVES TREADING CAUTIOUSLY DOWN THE STEPS TO THE CELLAR IN WHICH THE CHESTER ALAN ARTHUR HAD BEEN CONSTRUCTED...
SEE YOU THAT, MY DEAR WINCHESTER?

"IT...IT APPEARS TO BE A **SHIP'S CRADLE** OF SOME SORT...

BUT THERE IS SCARCELY A **BODY** OF **WATER** IN THIS COUNTY...

"...AND *THAT*, WINCHESTER, IS THE **CRUX** OF THE MATTER--AS DR. **CONAN DOYLE** WOULD REMARK, ' ELIMINATE THE **IMPOSSIBLE** AND THAT WHICH REMAINS IS **OBVIOUS.**'

...OR WORDS TO THAT MEANING...

SO....

...*IF* THAT WHICH WAS **BUILT** HERE IS **NOT** A **CRAFT** THAT SAILS UPON **WATER**, MAYHAP THE MEDIUM IS THE **UNIVERSAL AETHER** ITSELF!

WINCHESTER, IF WE CAN BUT LOCATE THE PROFESSOR'S **NOTEBOOKS**, NOW THAT THE SCHOOL TERM IS ABOUT TO END, WE WILL HAVE AMPLE FREE TIME NECESSARY TO **DUPLICATE** HIS CRAFT AND **FOLLOW** HIM UPON WHATEVER GREAT VENTURE HE HAS **UNDERTAKEN!**

GASP!

"**GASP!**" INDEED, DEAR READER, FOR AT THAT VERY MOMENT...

CHUF! CHUF!

STOKE HARDER, JEFFERSON, FOR WE ARE LOSING OUR HEAD OF STEAM!

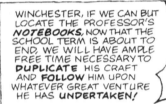

...THAT HARDY LITTLE CRAFT, THE *CHESTER ALAN ARTHUR*, WAS ENGAGED IN MAKING "PLANETARY MOORAGE," BLACK COAL SMOKE BILLOWING PROUDLY INTO THE ATMOSPHERE OF THE NEW WORLD...

WE WILL HOVER OVER THIS MEADOW, LADS!

ANCHOR DOWN, GENTLEMEN...

...AND TO **YOU**, HERKIMER, THE HONOR OF BEING THE **FIRST** TO DISEMBARK!

OH, JOY!

REMEMBER TO MAKE HASTE TO SIGNAL AT THE FIRST SIGHT OF HOSTILE ACTIVITY!

AYE AYE, SIR!

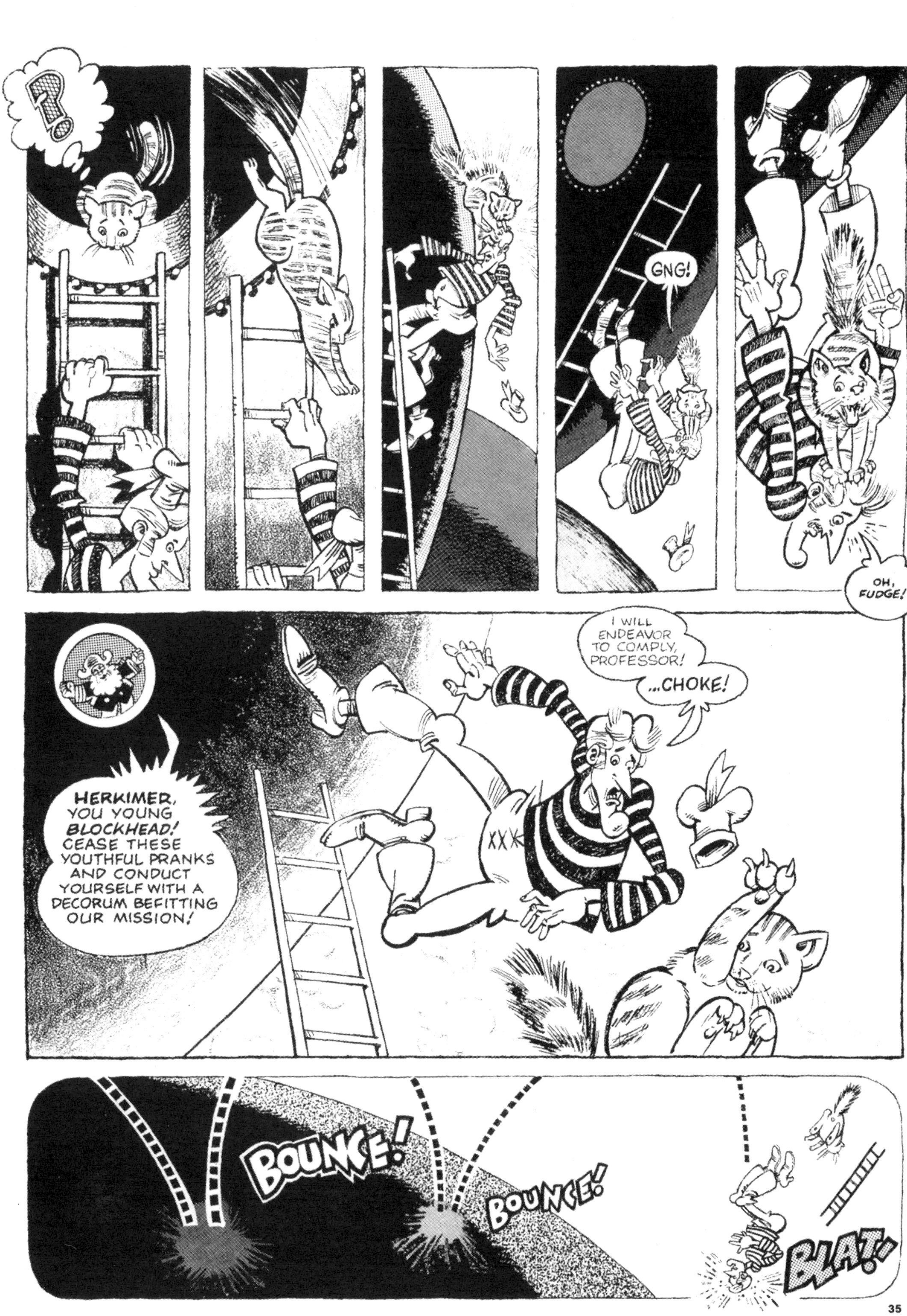
?
GNG!
OH, FUDGE!
I WILL ENDEAVOR TO COMPLY, PROFESSOR!
...CHOKE!
HERKIMER, YOU YOUNG BLOCKHEAD! CEASE THESE YOUTHFUL PRANKS AND CONDUCT YOURSELF WITH A DECORUM BEFITTING OUR MISSION!
BOUNCE!
BOUNCE!
BLAT!

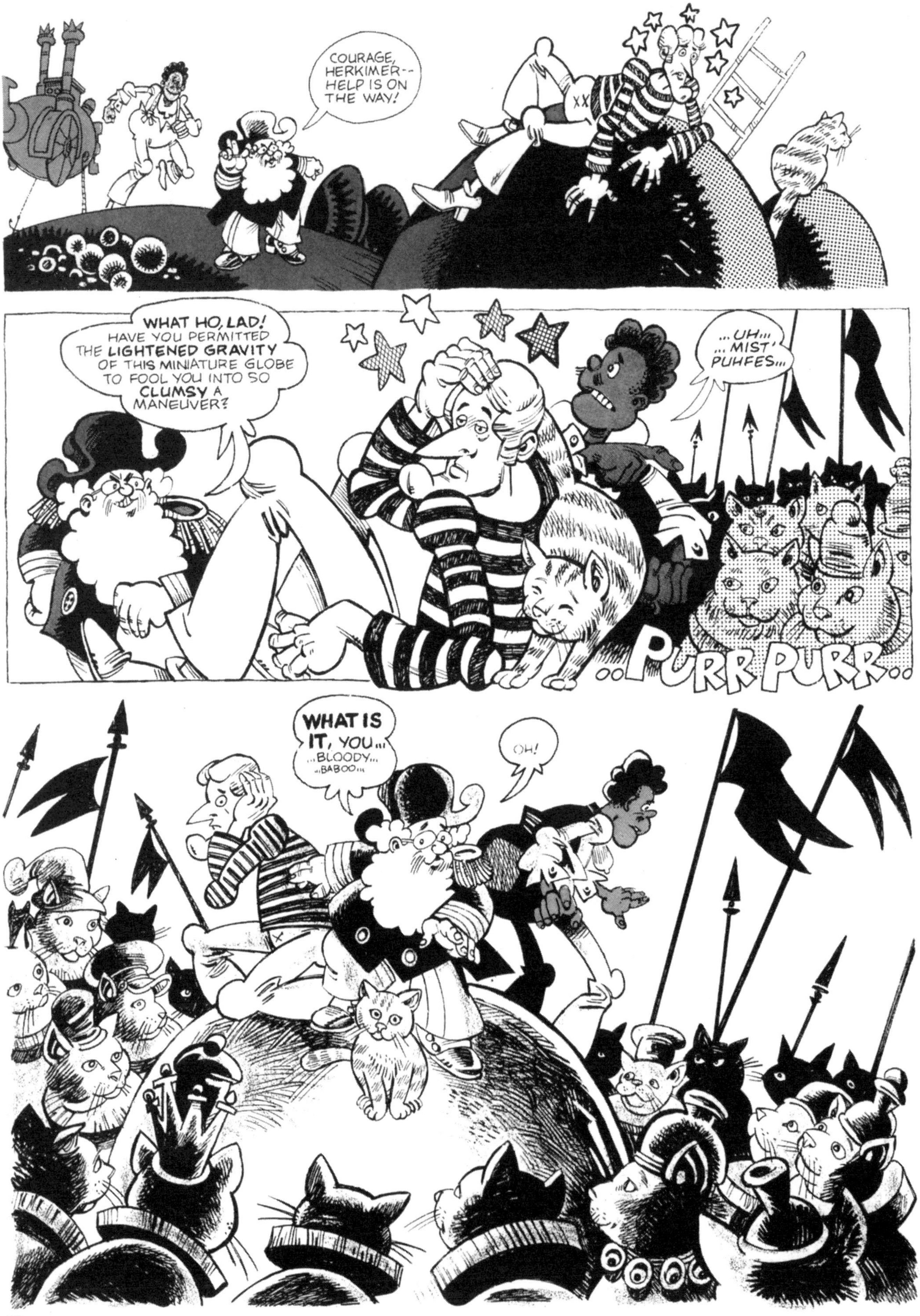

COURAGE, HERKIMER-- HELP IS ON THE WAY!
WHAT HO, LAD! HAVE YOU PERMITTED THE LIGHTENED GRAVITY OF THIS MINIATURE GLOBE TO FOOL YOU INTO SO CLUMSY A MANEUVER?
...UH... ...MIST' PUHFES...
..PURR PURR..
WHAT IS IT, YOU... ...BLOODY... ..BABOO...
OH!

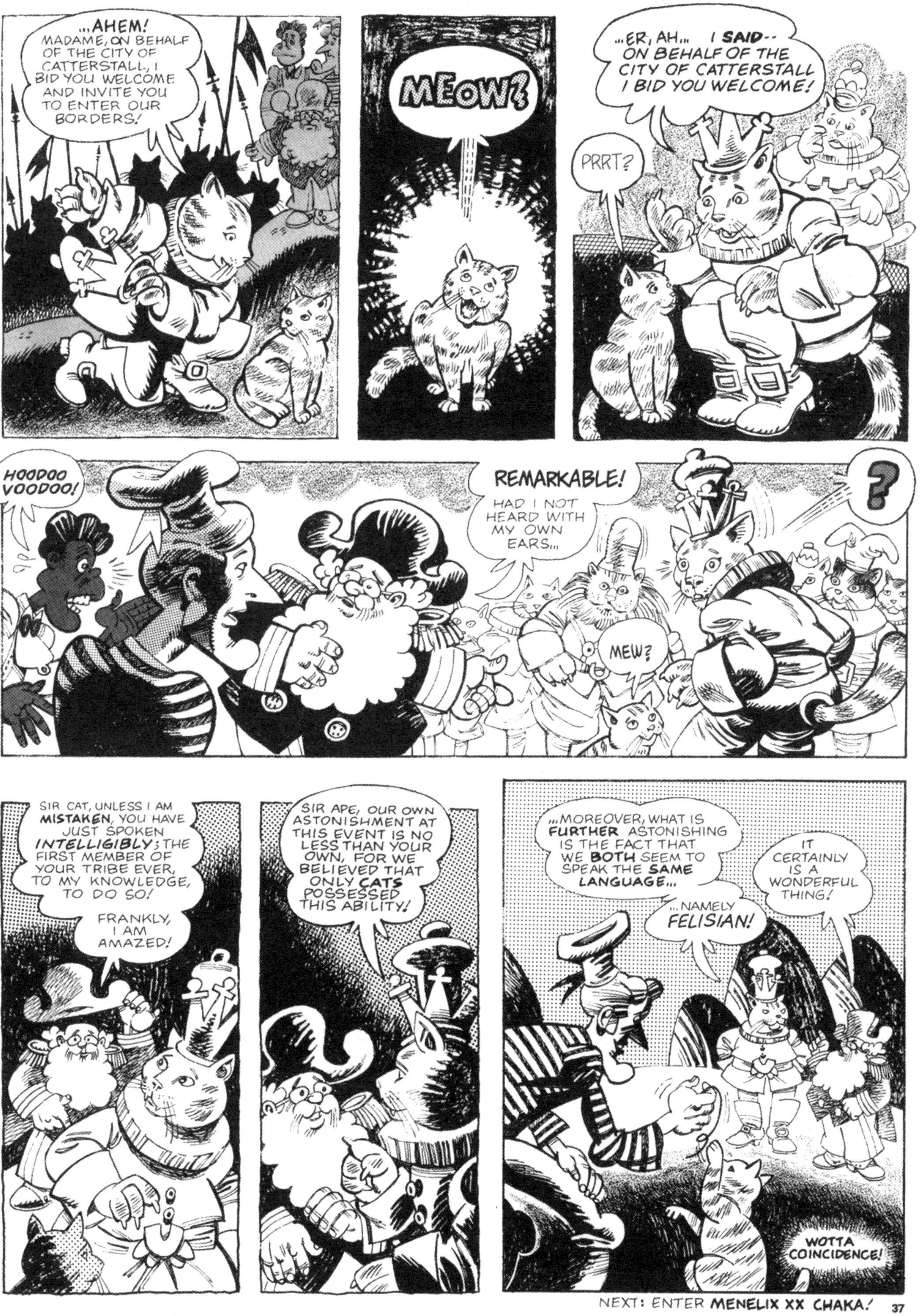
...AHEM! MADAME, ON BEHALF OF THE CITY OF CATTERSTALL, I BID YOU WELCOME AND INVITE YOU TO ENTER OUR BORDERS!
MEOW?
...ER, AH... I SAID-- ON BEHALF OF THE CITY OF CATTERSTALL I BID YOU WELCOME!
PRRT?
HOODOO VOODOO!
REMARKABLE!
HAD I NOT HEARD WITH MY OWN EARS...
?
MEW?
SIR CAT, UNLESS I AM MISTAKEN, YOU HAVE JUST SPOKEN INTELLIGIBLY; THE FIRST MEMBER OF YOUR TRIBE EVER, TO MY KNOWLEDGE, TO DO SO!
FRANKLY, I AM AMAZED!
SIR APE, OUR OWN ASTONISHMENT AT THIS EVENT IS NO LESS THAN YOUR OWN, FOR WE BELIEVED THAT ONLY CATS POSSESSED THIS ABILITY!
...MOREOVER, WHAT IS FURTHER ASTONISHING IS THE FACT THAT WE BOTH SEEM TO SPEAK THE SAME LANGUAGE...
...NAMELY FELISIAN!
IT CERTAINLY IS A WONDERFUL THING!
WOTTA COINCIDENCE!

THE ADVENTURES OF PROFESSOR THINTWHISTLE AND HIS INCREDIBLE AETHER FLYER

CHAPTER SEVEN

Perhaps this may strain common credibility, dear reader (dear, understanding, patient reader), *but*. . .having traversed the *Inner Aether* found within *SELENA* (Queen of the Moon!), and having encountered *Flying feathered Aztec serpents* and the like, our aether travelers have made moorage upon the planet Felisia-aleph, a globe inhabited by sentient, talking *cats!* Imagine their surprise!

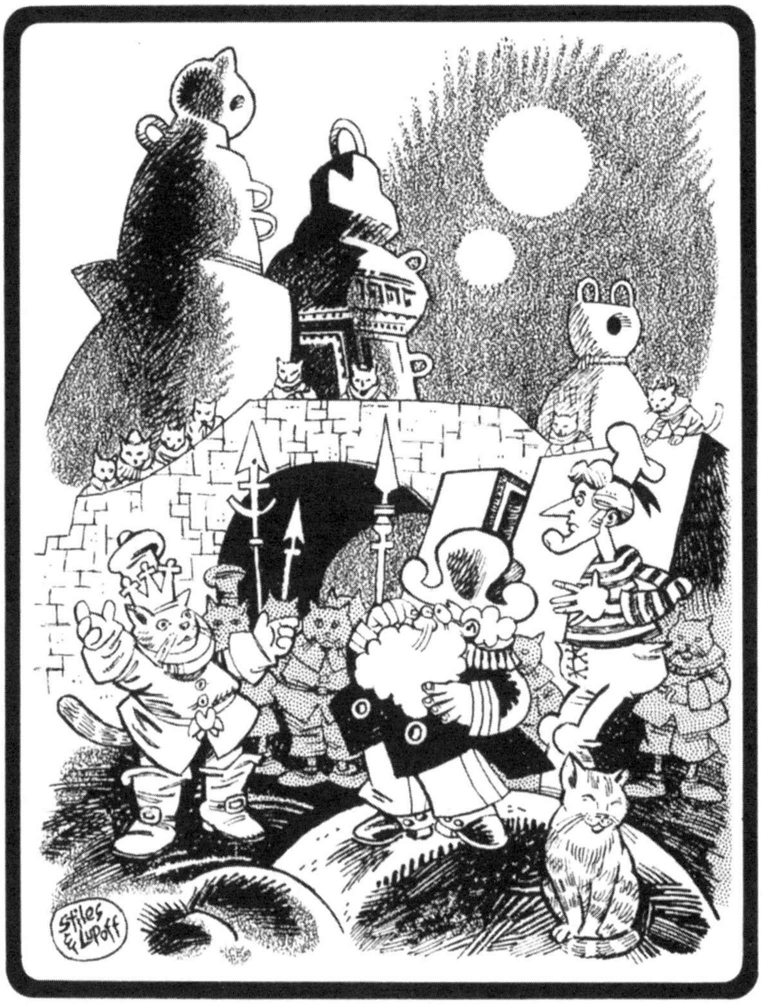

Stiles & Lupoff

HOW TO *BEGIN* TO DESCRIBE THE WONDERMENT OF CATTERSTALL, FELINE CAPITAL OF FELISIA-ALEPH?

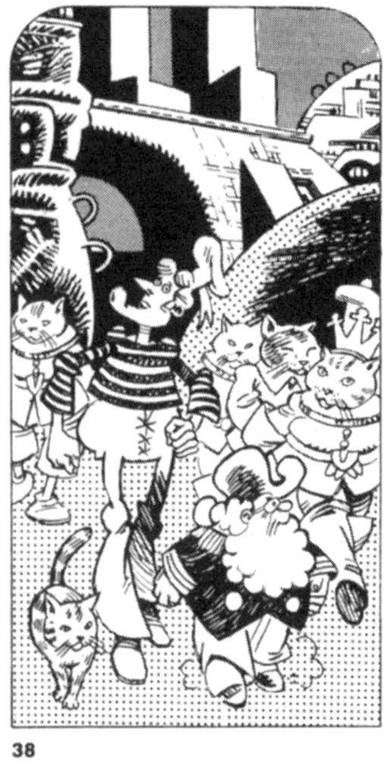

TO ENCOMPASS THIS MARVEL WOULD IT SUFFICE TO SAY THAT THE ARCHITECTURE BORE LITTLE IN COMMON WITH THAT OF BUFFALO FALLS, PA.?

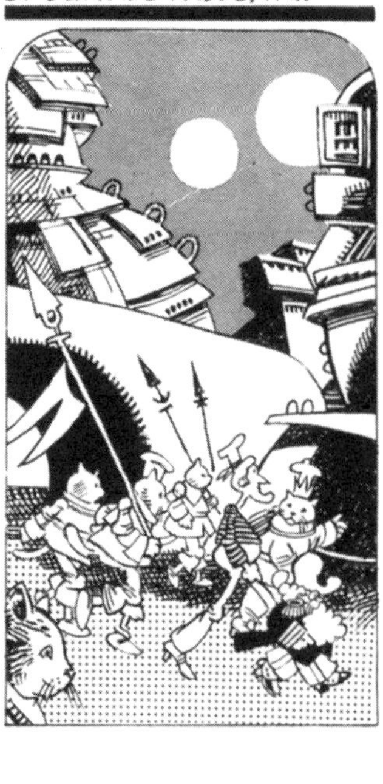

...OR OF EAST LIVERPOOL, OHIO? OF PARTICULAR NOTE WAS THE PRESENCE ON THE SIDEWALKS, IN RANKS UPON THE BOULEVARDS, AND EVEN UPON THE LEDGES OF THE BUILDINGS, OF A VERY LARGE NUMBER OF **CROQUET WICKETS.**

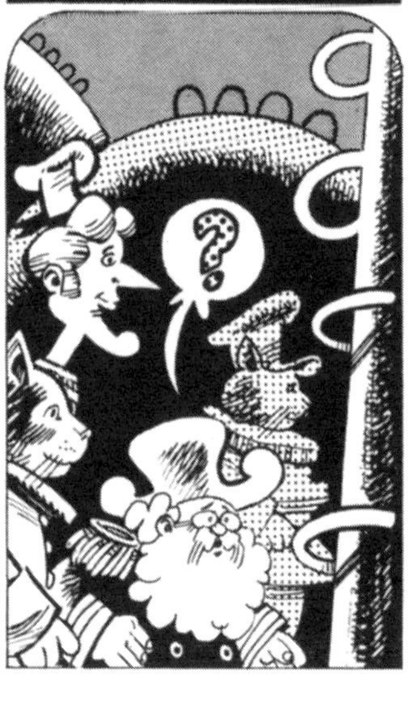

?

AT *PRECISELY* THE MOMENT OF THE PROFESSOR'S NOTICE OF THIS **SIGNAL ODDITY** THERE WAS HEARD RADIATING FROM THE TOPS OF THE BUILDINGS OF THE CAT CITY A SOUND **UNPRECEDENTED** IN THE EXPERIENCE OF THE AETHER TRAVELERS, AS IF THE STRAINS OF A **MULTIPLICITY** OF GUITAR STRINGS WERE BEING **AMPLIFIED** THROUGH SOME **GIGANTIC MEGAPHONE!**

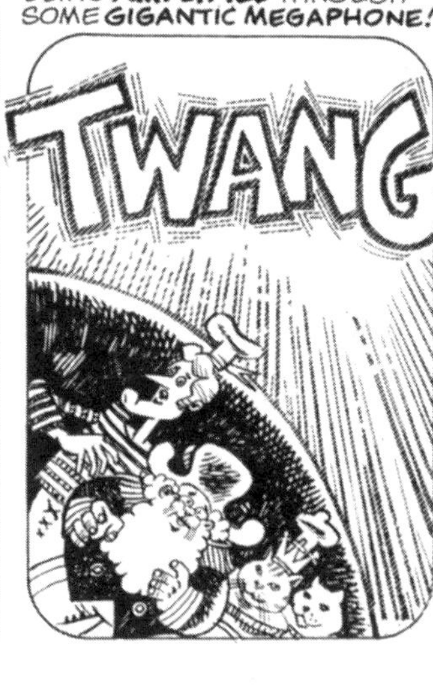

TWANG

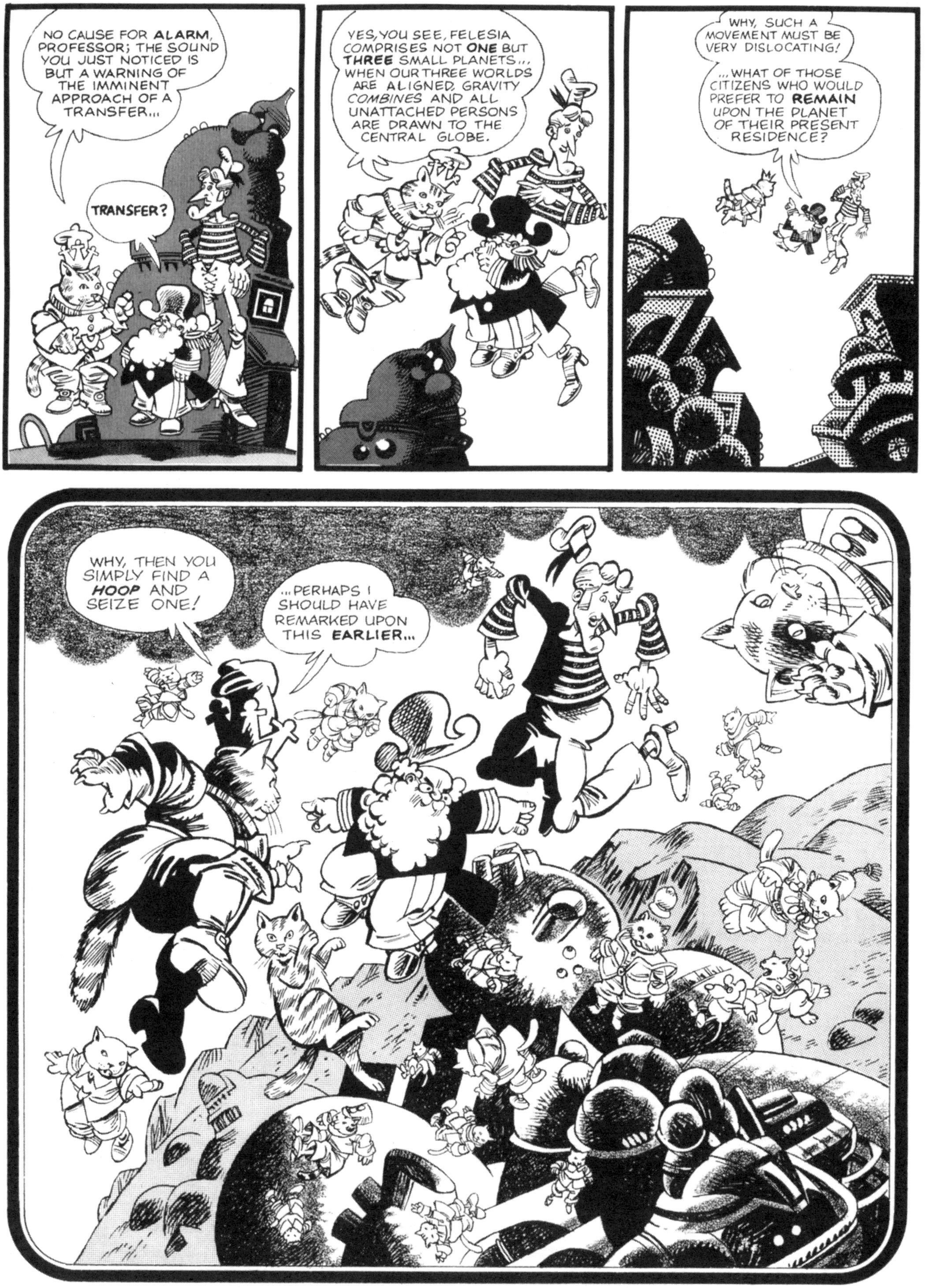
NO CAUSE FOR ALARM, PROFESSOR; THE SOUND YOU JUST NOTICED IS BUT A WARNING OF THE IMMINENT APPROACH OF A TRANSFER...
TRANSFER?
YES, YOU SEE, FELESIA COMPRISES NOT ONE BUT THREE SMALL PLANETS... WHEN OUR THREE WORLDS ARE ALIGNED, GRAVITY COMBINES AND ALL UNATTACHED PERSONS ARE DRAWN TO THE CENTRAL GLOBE.
WHY, SUCH A MOVEMENT MUST BE VERY DISLOCATING!
...WHAT OF THOSE CITIZENS WHO WOULD PREFER TO REMAIN UPON THE PLANET OF THEIR PRESENT RESIDENCE?
WHY, THEN YOU SIMPLY FIND A HOOP AND SEIZE ONE!
...PERHAPS I SHOULD HAVE REMARKED UPON THIS EARLIER...

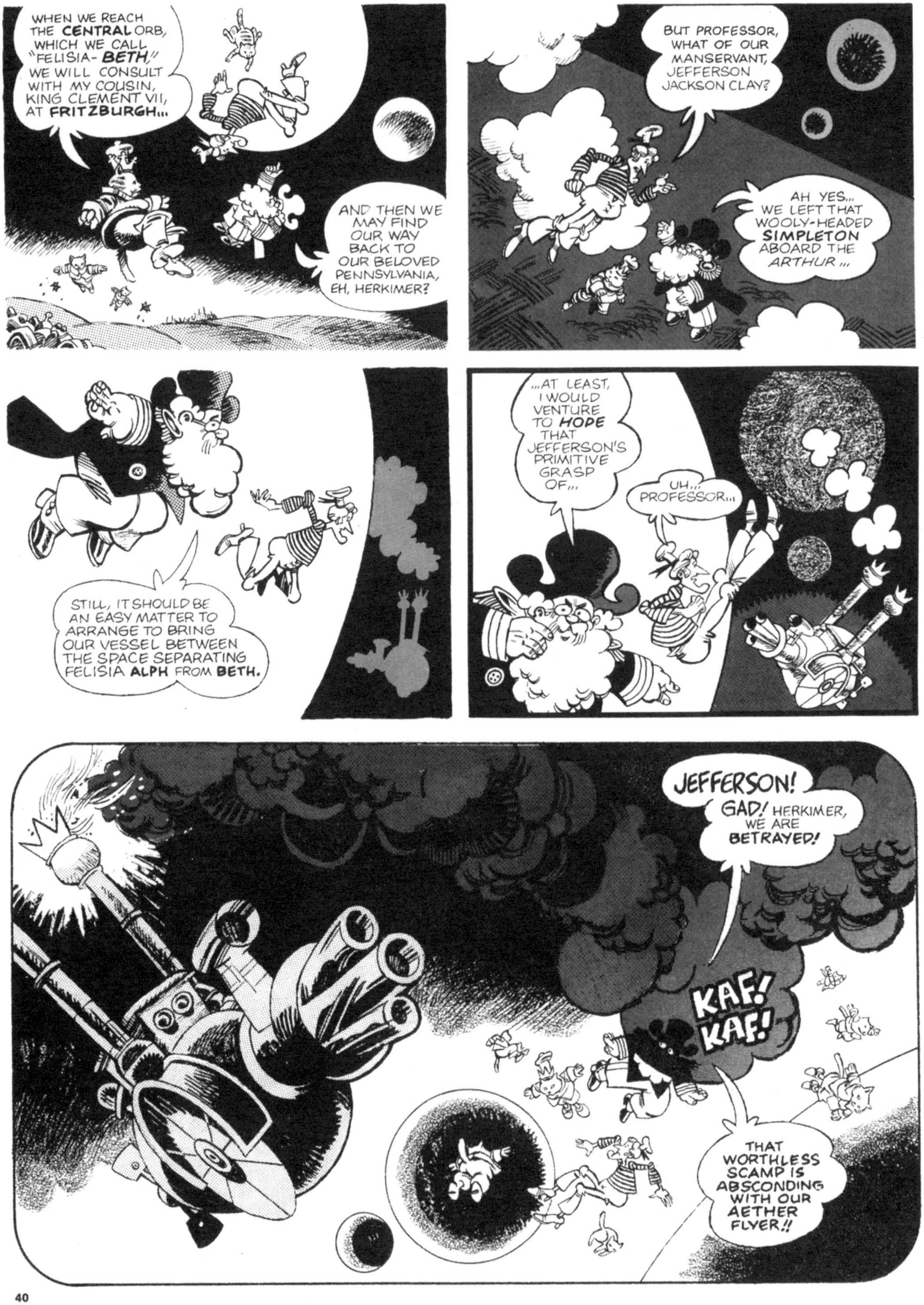
WHEN WE REACH THE CENTRAL ORB, WHICH WE CALL "FELISIA-BETH," WE WILL CONSULT WITH MY COUSIN, KING CLEMENT VII, AT FRITZBURGH...
AND THEN WE MAY FIND OUR WAY BACK TO OUR BELOVED PENNSYLVANIA, EH, HERKIMER?
BUT PROFESSOR, WHAT OF OUR MANSERVANT, JEFFERSON JACKSON CLAY?
AH YES... WE LEFT THAT WOOLY-HEADED SIMPLETON ABOARD THE ARTHUR...
STILL, IT SHOULD BE AN EASY MATTER TO ARRANGE TO BRING OUR VESSEL BETWEEN THE SPACE SEPARATING FELISIA ALPH FROM BETH.
...AT LEAST, I WOULD VENTURE TO HOPE THAT JEFFERSON'S PRIMITIVE GRASP OF...
UH... PROFESSOR...
JEFFERSON!
GAD! HERKIMER, WE ARE BETRAYED!
KAF! KAF!
THAT WORTHLESS SCAMP IS ABSCONDING WITH OUR AETHER FLYER!!

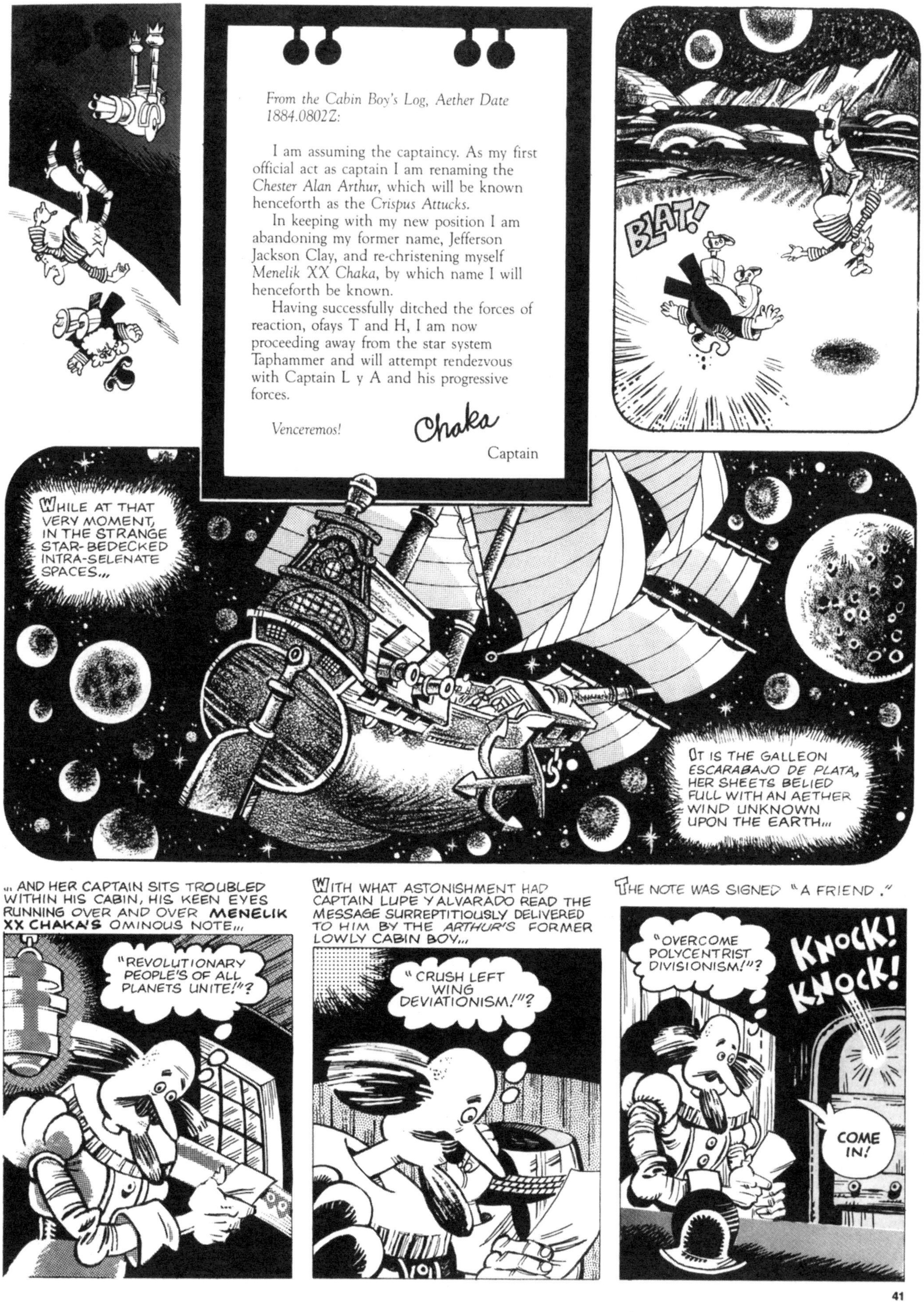
From the Cabin Boy's Log, Aether Date 1884.0802Z:
I am assuming the captaincy. As my first official act as captain I am renaming the Chester Alan Arthur, which will be known henceforth as the Crispus Attucks.
In keeping with my new position I am abandoning my former name, Jefferson Jackson Clay, and re-christening myself Menelik XX Chaka, by which name I will henceforth be known.
Having successfully ditched the forces of reaction, ofays T and H, I am now proceeding away from the star system Taphammer and will attempt rendezvous with Captain L y A and his progressive forces.
Venceremos!
Chaka
Captain
BLAT!
WHILE AT THAT VERY MOMENT, IN THE STRANGE STAR-BEDECKED INTRA-SELENATE SPACES...
IT IS THE GALLEON ESCARABAJO DE PLATA, HER SHEETS BELIED FULL WITH AN AETHER WIND UNKNOWN UPON THE EARTH...
... AND HER CAPTAIN SITS TROUBLED WITHIN HIS CABIN, HIS KEEN EYES RUNNING OVER AND OVER MENELIK XX CHAKA'S OMINOUS NOTE...
"REVOLUTIONARY PEOPLE'S OF ALL PLANETS UNITE!"?
WITH WHAT ASTONISHMENT HAD CAPTAIN LUPE Y ALVARADO READ THE MESSAGE SURREPTITIOUSLY DELIVERED TO HIM BY THE ARTHUR'S FORMER LOWLY CABIN BOY...
"CRUSH LEFT WING DEVIATIONISM!"?
THE NOTE WAS SIGNED "A FRIEND."
"OVERCOME POLYCENTRIST DIVISIONISM!"?
KNOCK! KNOCK!
COME IN!

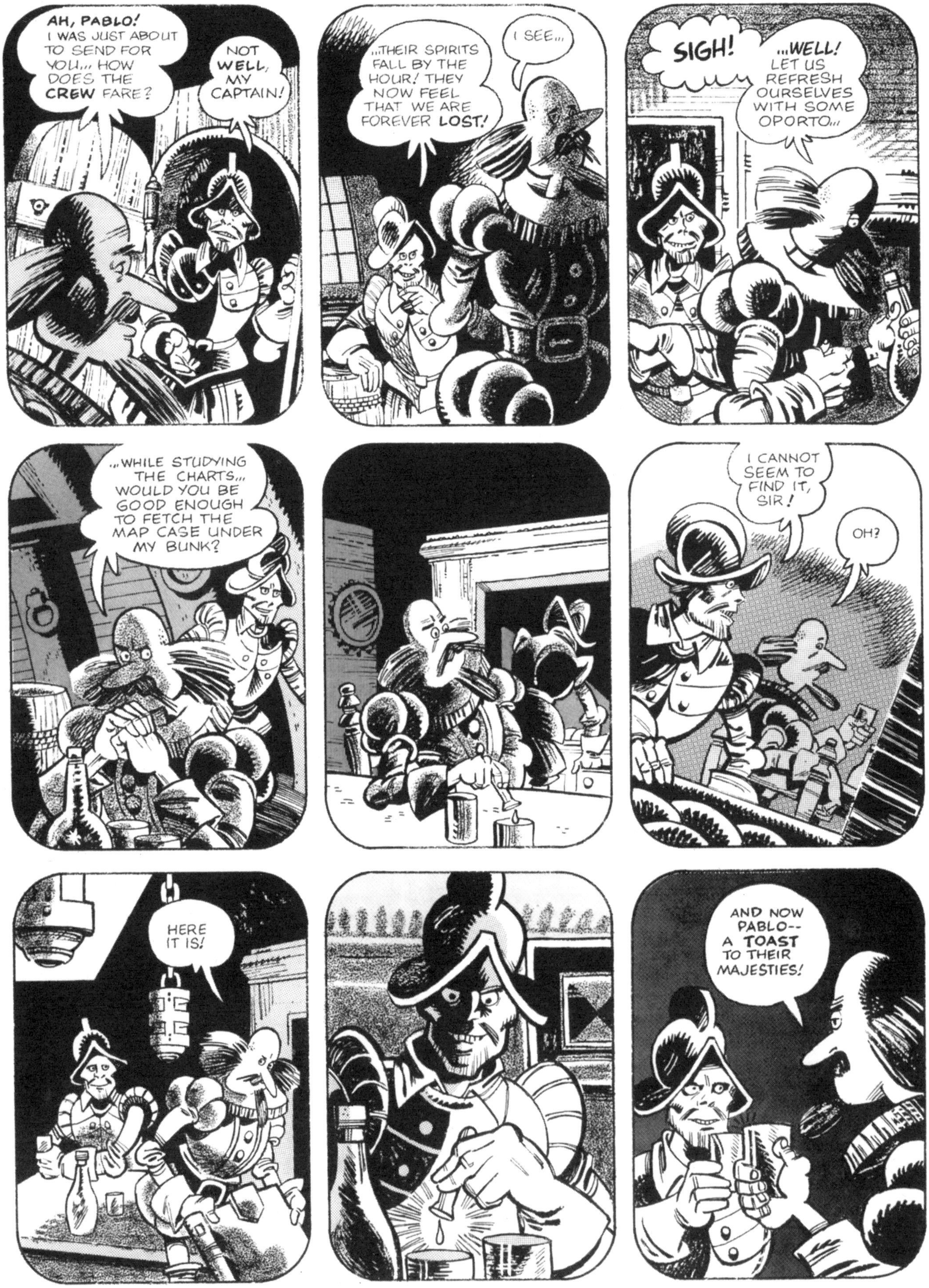
AH, PABLO! I WAS JUST ABOUT TO SEND FOR YOU... HOW DOES THE CREW FARE?
NOT WELL, MY CAPTAIN!
...THEIR SPIRITS FALL BY THE HOUR! THEY NOW FEEL THAT WE ARE FOREVER LOST!
I SEE...
SIGH!
...WELL! LET US REFRESH OURSELVES WITH SOME OPORTO...
...WHILE STUDYING THE CHARTS... WOULD YOU BE GOOD ENOUGH TO FETCH THE MAP CASE UNDER MY BUNK?
I CANNOT SEEM TO FIND IT, SIR!
OH?
HERE IT IS!
AND NOW PABLO-- A TOAST TO THEIR MAJESTIES!

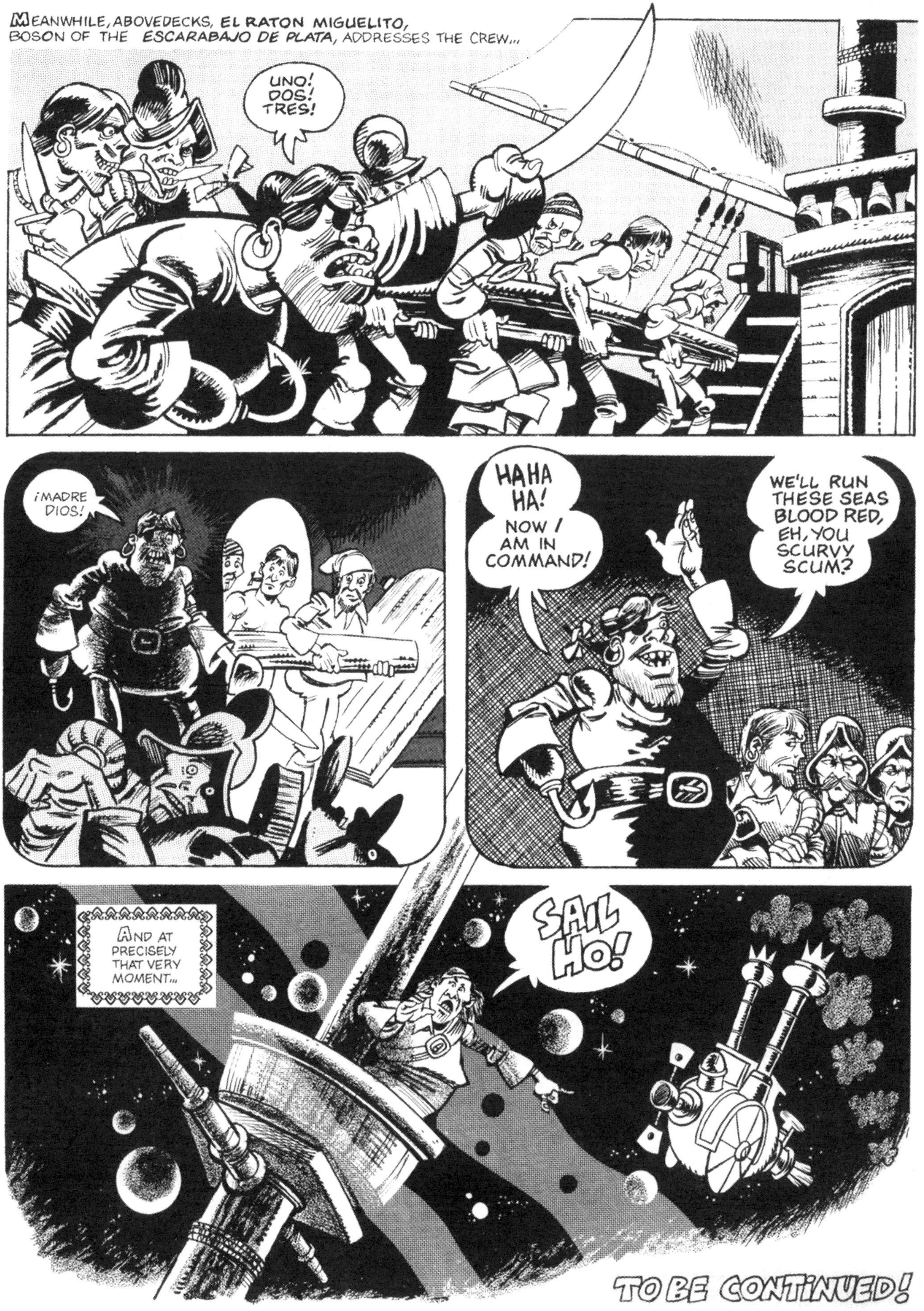
MEANWHILE, ABOVEDECKS, EL RATON MIGUELITO, BOSON OF THE ESCARABAJO DE PLATA, ADDRESSES THE CREW...
UNO! DOS! TRES!
¡MADRE DIOS!
HAHA HA! NOW I AM IN COMMAND!
WE'LL RUN THESE SEAS BLOOD RED, EH, YOU SCURVY SCUM?
AND AT PRECISELY THAT VERY MOMENT...
SAIL HO!
TO BE CONTINUED!

THE ADVENTURES OF PROFESSOR THINTWHISTLE AND HIS INCREDIBLE AETHER FLYER

Chapter Eight

There can be little dispute, reader, touching upon the singular events of the past chapter, that actual fact is often as confounding as fantasies commonly found in the pages of *Mark the Match Boy*. For no sooner had *Professor Theobald Uriah Thintwhistle* and his youthful companion *Herkimer* established contact with the feline inhabitants of Felisia *ALEPH* than the other two planets of the Felisia family, *Beth* and *Gemmel*, fell into Spatial Alignment. When this transpires, all cats and otherwise loose objects on the face of the *outer* planets are drawn by complex gravitational forces to the central orb (and why bore the reader with the mechanics of this phenomenon?). In this manner the three planets of Felisia periodically shift population from one to another, assuring the cultural continuity of the great people of the Felisian system. If the Professor and Herkimer were discomfited by this experience, one can only imagine the depths of their discomposure upon the discovery of the theft of the *Chester Alan Arthur*, "liberated" by *Menelik XX Chaka* (formerly *Jefferson Jackson Clay*, in a mighty blow to the forces of white colonial imperialism!

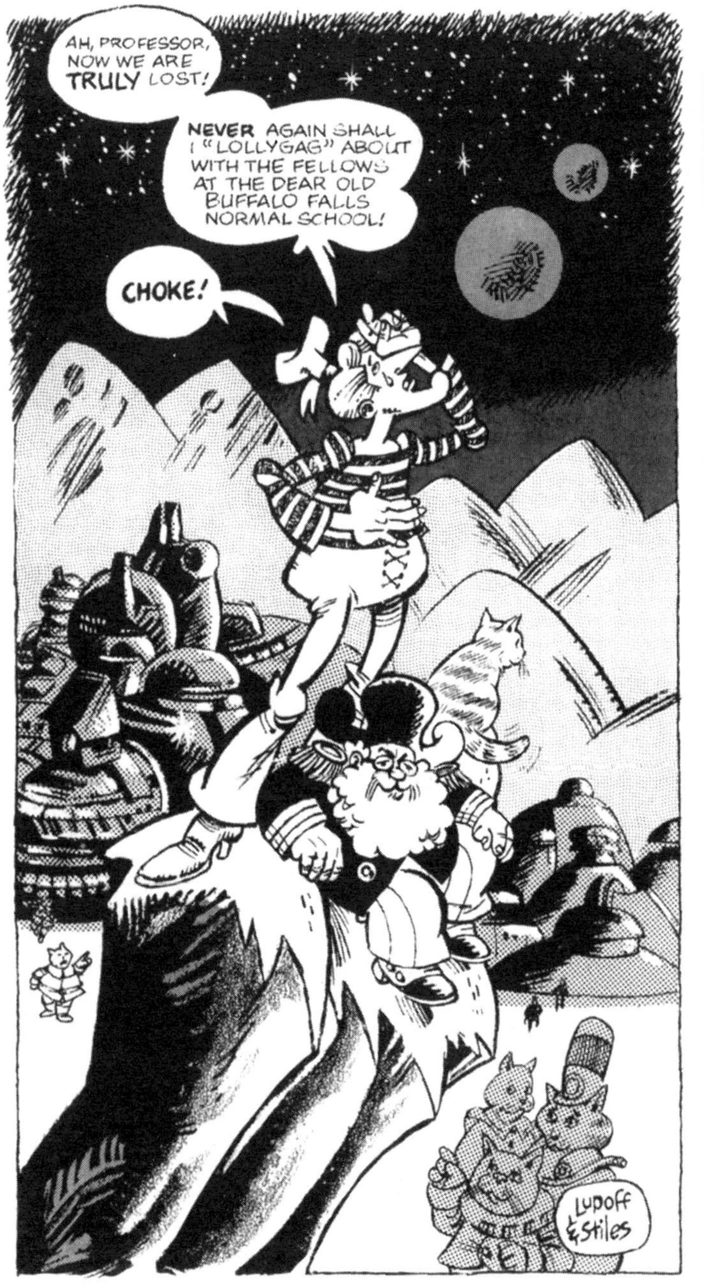
AH, PROFESSOR, NOW WE ARE TRULY LOST!
NEVER AGAIN SHALL I "LOLLYGAG" ABOUT WITH THE FELLOWS AT THE DEAR OLD BUFFALO FALLS NORMAL SCHOOL!
CHOKE!
LUPOFF & STILES

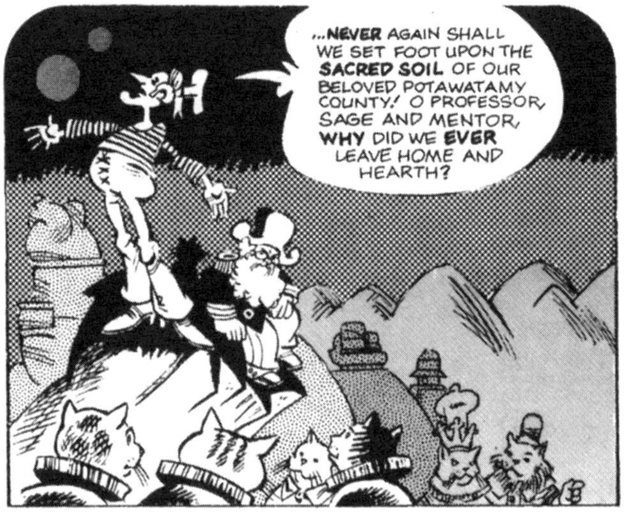
...NEVER AGAIN SHALL WE SET FOOT UPON THE SACRED SOIL OF OUR BELOVED POTAWATAMY COUNTY! O PROFESSOR, SAGE AND MENTOR, WHY DID WE EVER LEAVE HOME AND HEARTH?

WITH THIS PITEOUS ORATION, DELIVERED IN COMPANY OF FACIAL EXPRESSIONS AND MANUAL GESTICULATIONS CAREFULLY LEARNED IN THE NORMAL SCHOOL'S DRAMATIC DECLAMATION SYLLABUS, THE POOR LAD COLLAPSED INTO A RENEWED FRESHET OF TEARS.

WHAT THOUGHTS OCCUPIED THE SAVANT'S CRANIUM AT THAT MOMENT WE KNOW **NOT**, ALTHOUGH WE HAVE IN THE PAST DETECTED UNKIND NOTIONS UPON HIS PART AS DIRECTED TOWARD THE SIMPLE, YET EARNEST, YOUTH.

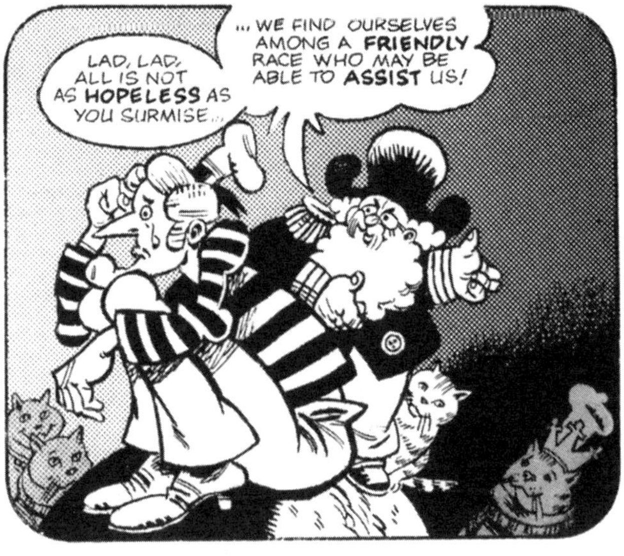
LAD, LAD, ALL IS NOT AS HOPELESS AS YOU SURMISE...
...WE FIND OURSELVES AMONG A FRIENDLY RACE WHO MAY BE ABLE TO ASSIST US!

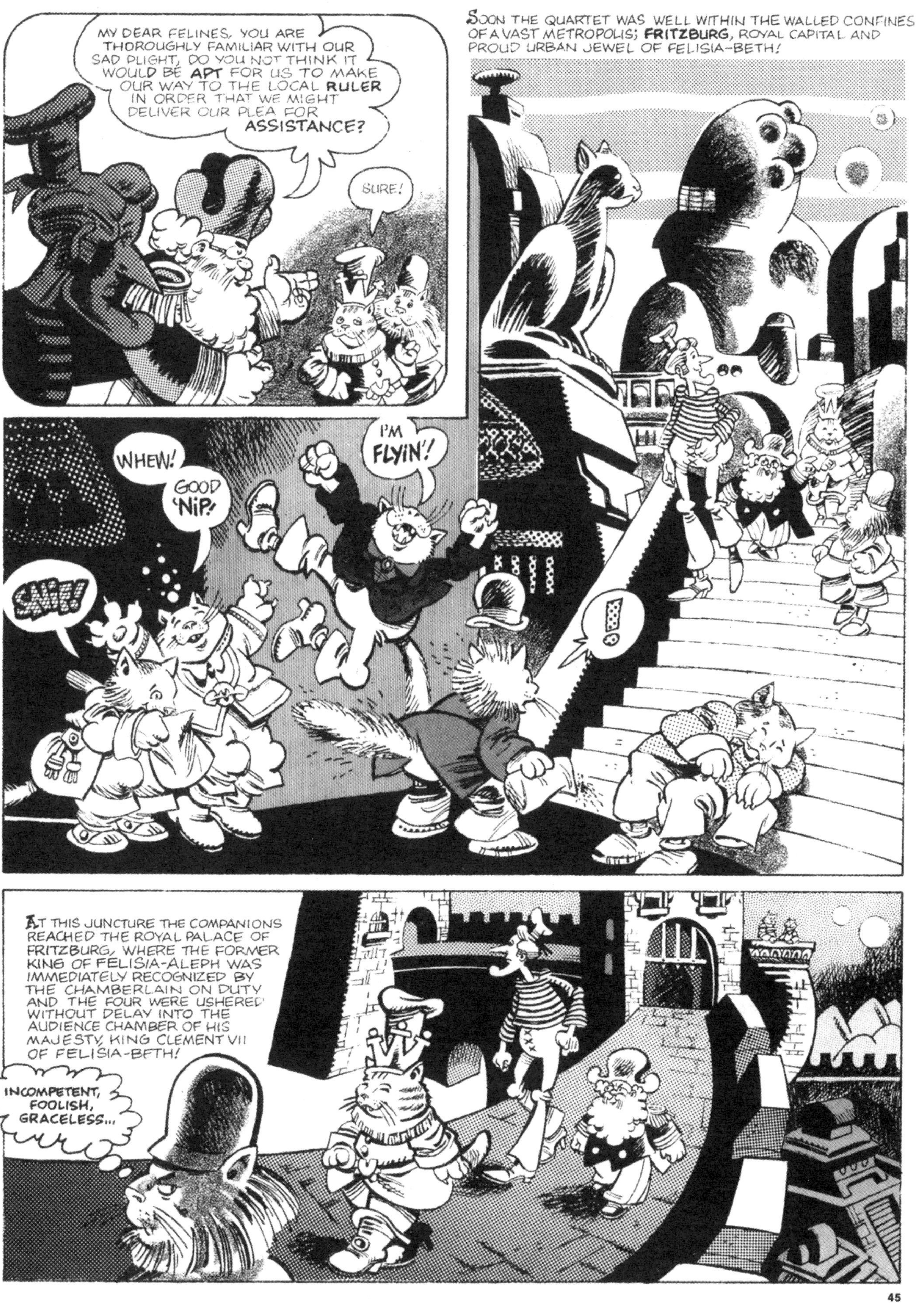

MY DEAR FELINES, YOU ARE THOROUGHLY FAMILIAR WITH OUR SAD PLIGHT, DO YOU NOT THINK IT WOULD BE APT FOR US TO MAKE OUR WAY TO THE LOCAL RULER IN ORDER THAT WE MIGHT DELIVER OUR PLEA FOR ASSISTANCE?
SURE!
SOON THE QUARTET WAS WELL WITHIN THE WALLED CONFINES OF A VAST METROPOLIS; FRITZBURG, ROYAL CAPITAL AND PROUD URBAN JEWEL OF FELISIA-BETH!
WHEW!
GOOD 'NIP!
I'M FLYIN'!
SNIF!
!
AT THIS JUNCTURE THE COMPANIONS REACHED THE ROYAL PALACE OF FRITZBURG, WHERE THE FORMER KING OF FELISIA-ALEPH WAS IMMEDIATELY RECOGNIZED BY THE CHAMBERLAIN ON DUTY AND THE FOUR WERE USHERED WITHOUT DELAY INTO THE AUDIENCE CHAMBER OF HIS MAJESTY, KING CLEMENT VII OF FELISIA-BETH!
INCOMPETENT, FOOLISH, GRACELESS...

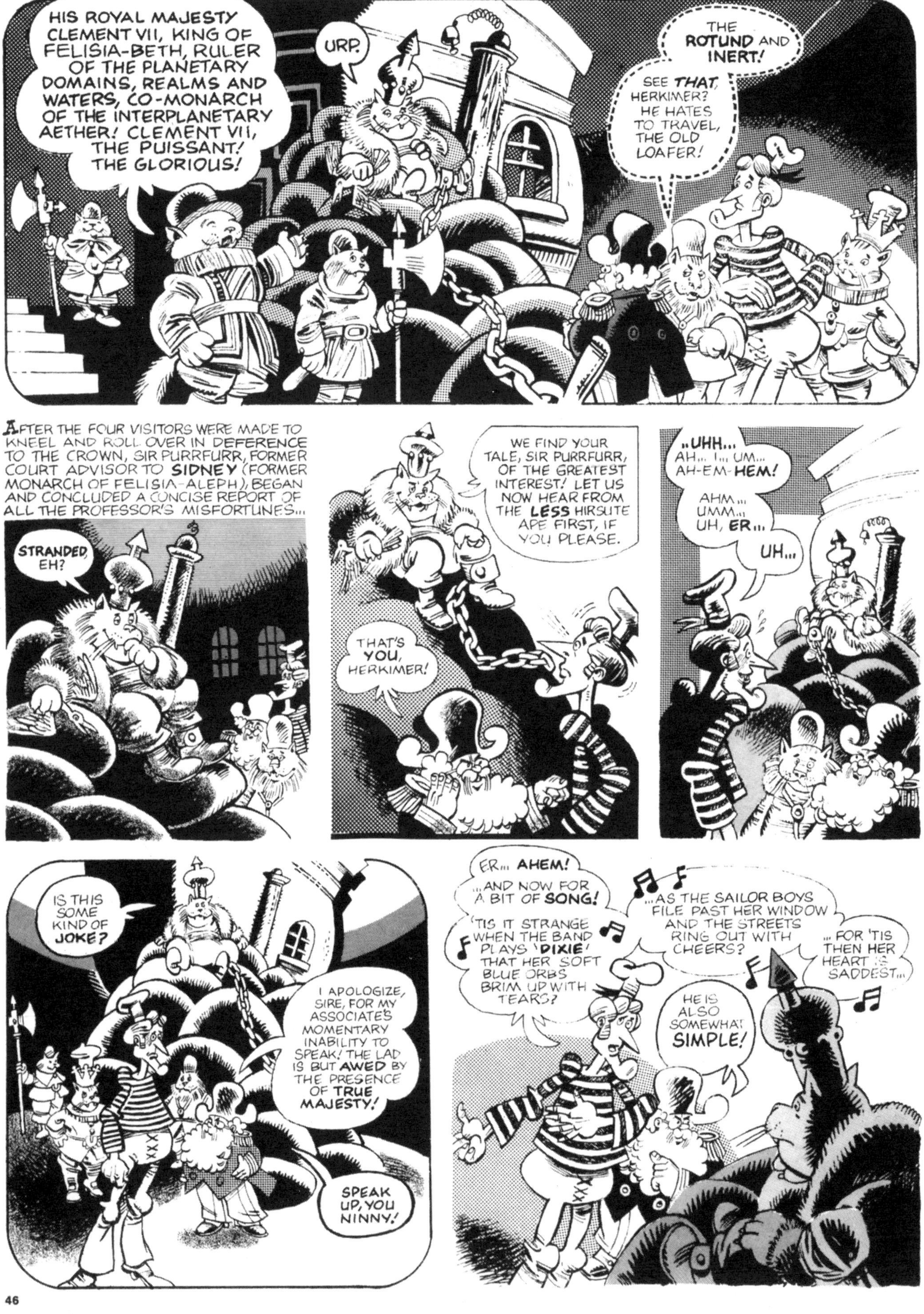
HIS ROYAL MAJESTY CLEMENT VII, KING OF FELISIA-BETH, RULER OF THE PLANETARY DOMAINS, REALMS AND WATERS, CO-MONARCH OF THE INTERPLANETARY AETHER! CLEMENT VII, THE PUISSANT! THE GLORIOUS!
URP.
THE ROTUND AND INERT!
SEE THAT, HERKIMER? HE HATES TO TRAVEL, THE OLD LOAFER!
AFTER THE FOUR VISITORS WERE MADE TO KNEEL AND ROLL OVER IN DEFERENCE TO THE CROWN, SIR PURRFURR, FORMER COURT ADVISOR TO SIDNEY (FORMER MONARCH OF FELISIA-ALEPH), BEGAN AND CONCLUDED A CONCISE REPORT OF ALL THE PROFESSOR'S MISFORTUNES...
STRANDED, EH?
WE FIND YOUR TALE, SIR PURRFURR, OF THE GREATEST INTEREST! LET US NOW HEAR FROM THE LESS HIRSUTE APE FIRST, IF YOU PLEASE.
THAT'S YOU, HERKIMER!
..UHH... AH... I... UM... AH-EM-HEM!
AHM... UMM... UH, ER...
UH...
IS THIS SOME KIND OF JOKE?
I APOLOGIZE, SIRE, FOR MY ASSOCIATE'S MOMENTARY INABILITY TO SPEAK! THE LAD IS BUT AWED BY THE PRESENCE OF TRUE MAJESTY!
SPEAK UP, YOU NINNY!
ER... AHEM!
...AND NOW FOR A BIT OF SONG!
'TIS IT STRANGE WHEN THE BAND PLAYS 'DIXIE' THAT HER SOFT BLUE ORBS BRIM UP WITH TEARS?
...AS THE SAILOR BOYS FILE PAST HER WINDOW AND THE STREETS RING OUT WITH CHEERS?
... FOR 'TIS THEN HER HEART IS SADDEST...
HE IS ALSO SOMEWHAT SIMPLE!

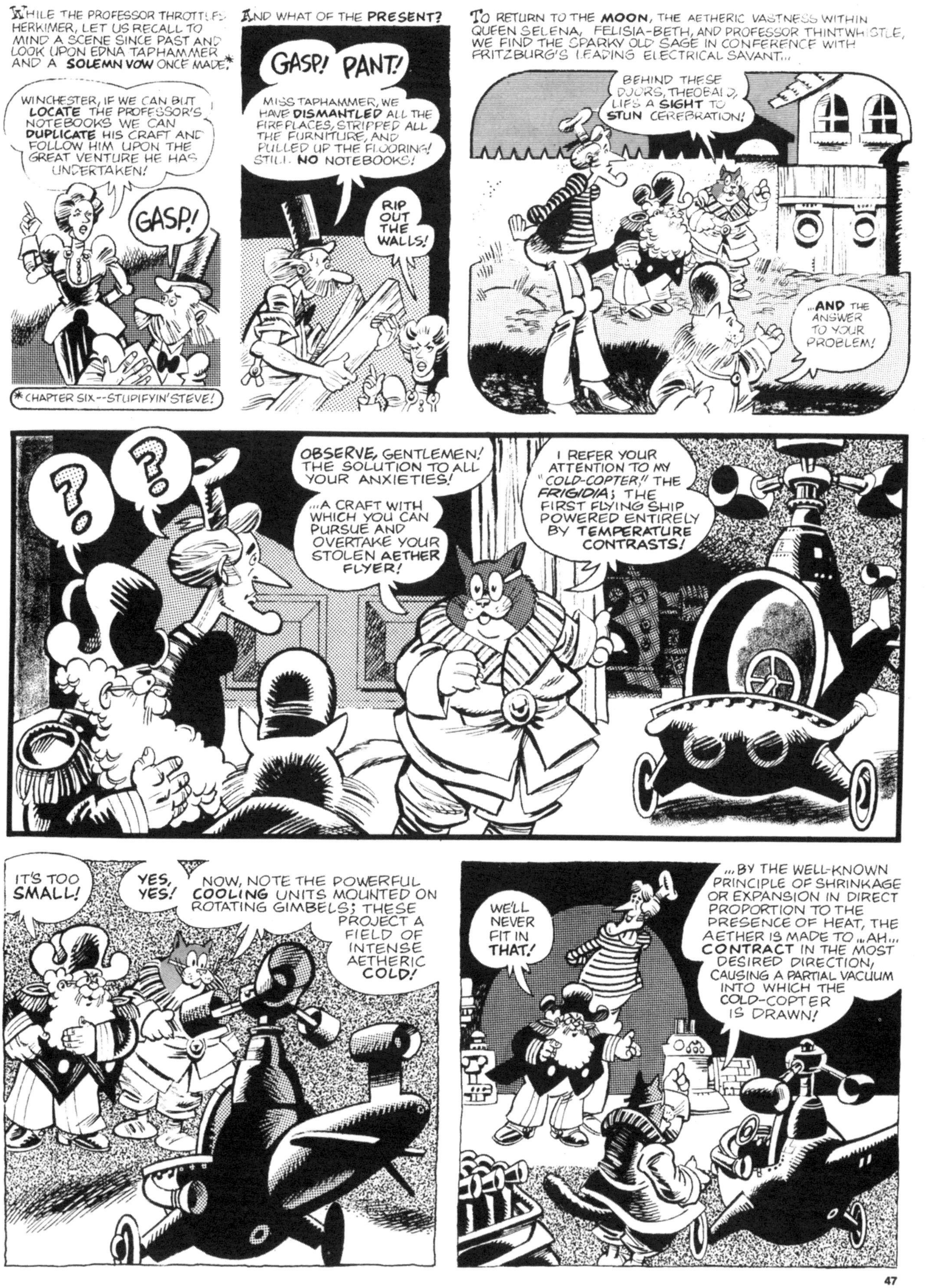
WHILE THE PROFESSOR THROTTLES HERKIMER, LET US RECALL TO MIND A SCENE SINCE PAST AND LOOK UPON EDNA TAPHAMMER AND A SOLEMN VOW ONCE MADE!*
WINCHESTER, IF WE CAN BUT LOCATE THE PROFESSOR'S NOTEBOOKS WE CAN DUPLICATE HIS CRAFT AND FOLLOW HIM UPON THE GREAT VENTURE HE HAS UNDERTAKEN!
GASP!
*CHAPTER SIX--STUPIFYIN' STEVE!
AND WHAT OF THE PRESENT?
GASP! PANT!
MISS TAPHAMMER, WE HAVE DISMANTLED ALL THE FIREPLACES, STRIPPED ALL THE FURNITURE, AND PULLED UP THE FLOORING! STILL NO NOTEBOOKS!
RIP OUT THE WALLS!
TO RETURN TO THE MOON, THE AETHERIC VASTNESS WITHIN QUEEN SELENA, FELISIA-BETH, AND PROFESSOR THINTWHISTLE, WE FIND THE SPARKY OLD SAGE IN CONFERENCE WITH FRITZBURG'S LEADING ELECTRICAL SAVANT...
BEHIND THESE DOORS, THEOBALD, LIES A SIGHT TO STUN CEREBRATION!
...AND THE ANSWER TO YOUR PROBLEM!
?
?
OBSERVE, GENTLEMEN! THE SOLUTION TO ALL YOUR ANXIETIES!
...A CRAFT WITH WHICH YOU CAN PURSUE AND OVERTAKE YOUR STOLEN AETHER FLYER!
I REFER YOUR ATTENTION TO MY "COLD-COPTER," THE FRIGIDIA; THE FIRST FLYING SHIP POWERED ENTIRELY BY TEMPERATURE CONTRASTS!
IT'S TOO SMALL!
YES, YES!
NOW, NOTE THE POWERFUL COOLING UNITS MOUNTED ON ROTATING GIMBELS; THESE PROJECT A FIELD OF INTENSE AETHERIC COLD!
WE'LL NEVER FIT IN THAT!
...BY THE WELL-KNOWN PRINCIPLE OF SHRINKAGE OR EXPANSION IN DIRECT PROPORTION TO THE PRESENCE OF HEAT, THE AETHER IS MADE TO ...AH... CONTRACT IN THE MOST DESIRED DIRECTION, CAUSING A PARTIAL VACUUM INTO WHICH THE COLD-COPTER IS DRAWN!

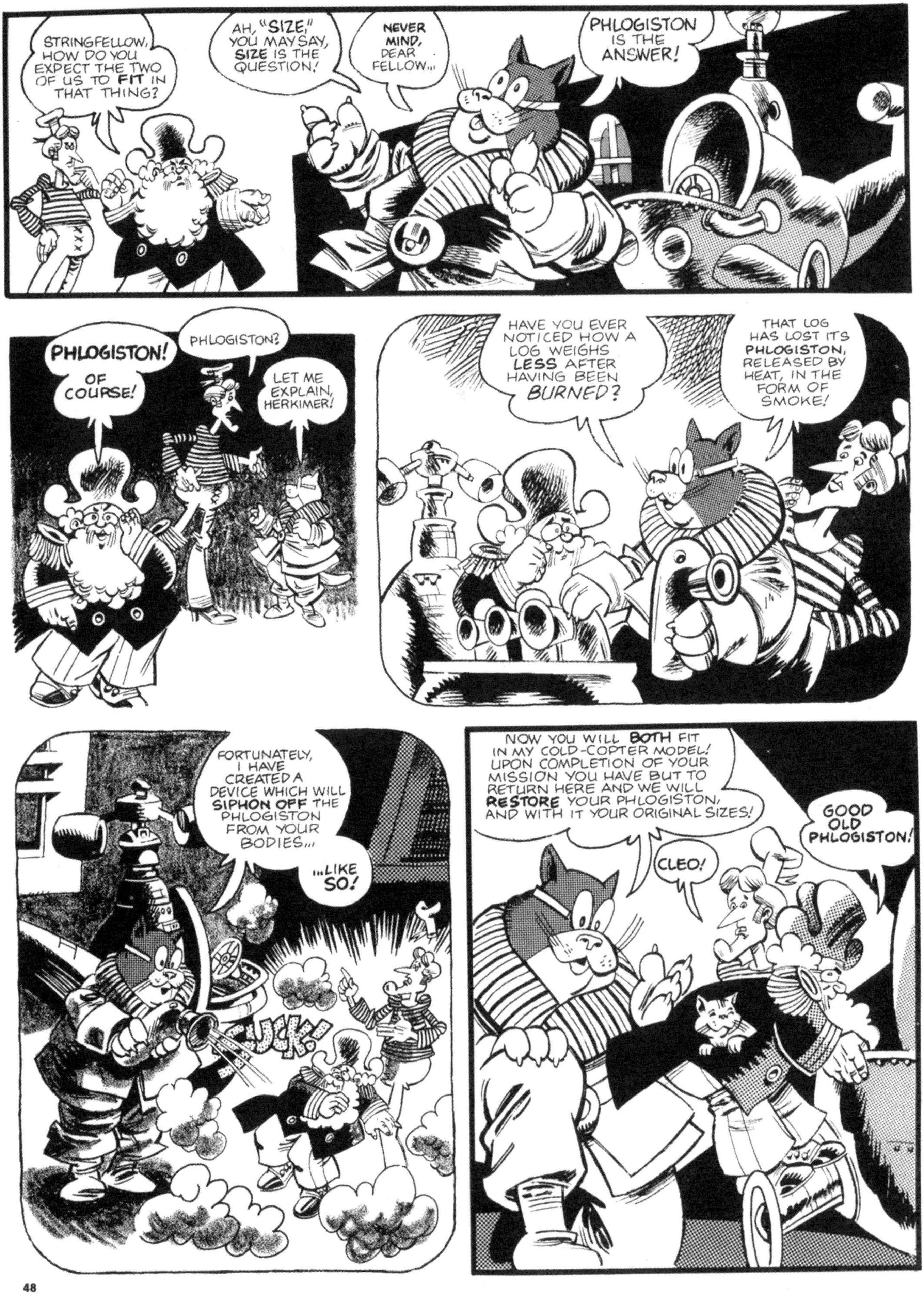

STRINGFELLOW, HOW DO YOU EXPECT THE TWO OF US TO FIT IN THAT THING?
AH, "SIZE," YOU MAY SAY, SIZE IS THE QUESTION!
NEVER MIND, DEAR FELLOW...
PHLOGISTON IS THE ANSWER!
PHLOGISTON!
OF COURSE!
PHLOGISTON?
LET ME EXPLAIN, HERKIMER!
HAVE YOU EVER NOTICED HOW A LOG WEIGHS LESS AFTER HAVING BEEN BURNED?
THAT LOG HAS LOST ITS PHLOGISTON, RELEASED BY HEAT, IN THE FORM OF SMOKE!
FORTUNATELY, I HAVE CREATED A DEVICE WHICH WILL SIPHON OFF THE PHLOGISTON FROM YOUR BODIES...
...LIKE SO!
SUCK!
NOW YOU WILL BOTH FIT IN MY COLD-COPTER MODEL! UPON COMPLETION OF YOUR MISSION YOU HAVE BUT TO RETURN HERE AND WE WILL RESTORE YOUR PHLOGISTON, AND WITH IT YOUR ORIGINAL SIZES!
CLEO!
GOOD OLD PHLOGISTON!

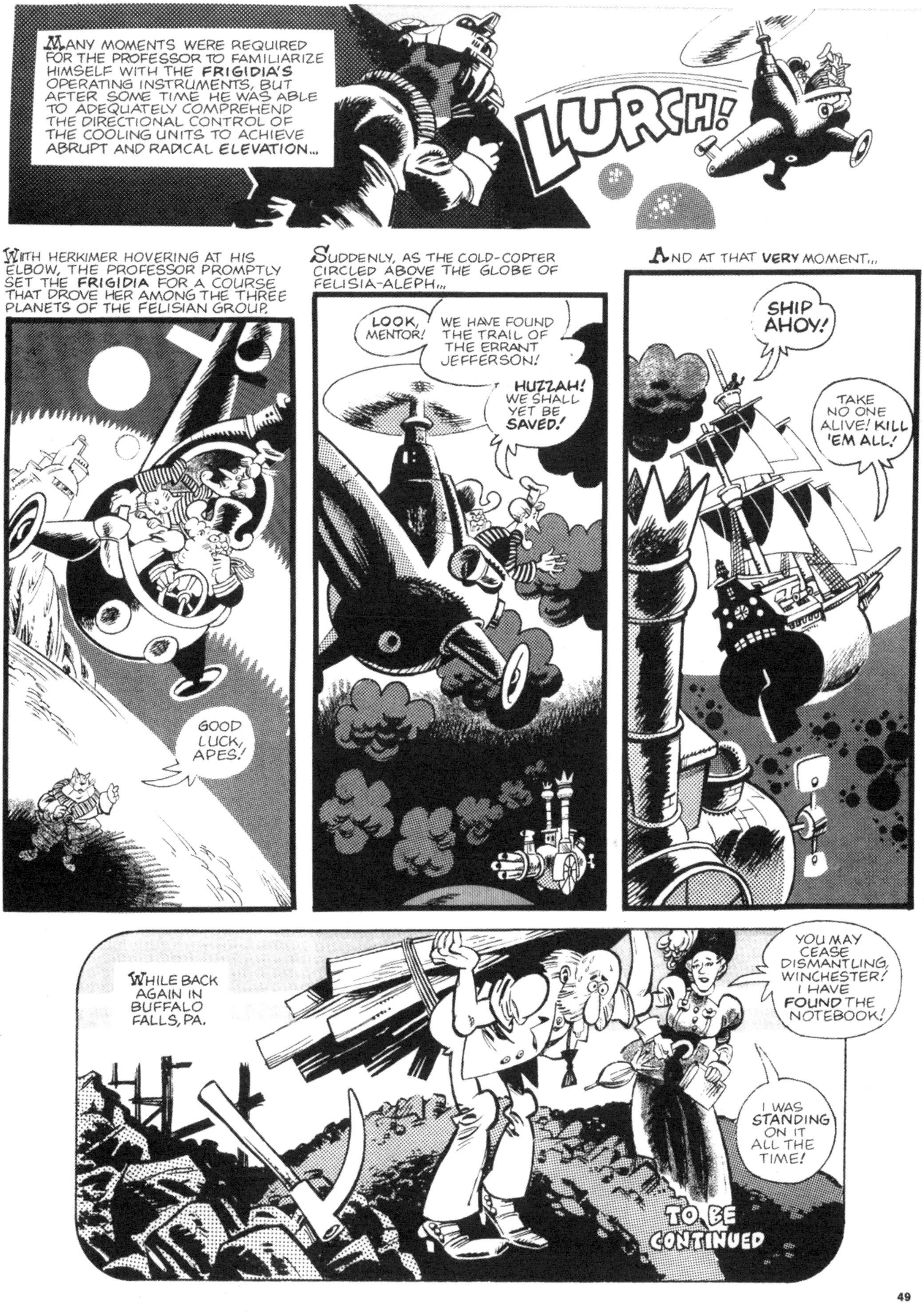

MANY MOMENTS WERE REQUIRED FOR THE PROFESSOR TO FAMILIARIZE HIMSELF WITH THE FRIGIDIA'S OPERATING INSTRUMENTS, BUT AFTER SOME TIME HE WAS ABLE TO ADEQUATELY COMPREHEND THE DIRECTIONAL CONTROL OF THE COOLING UNITS TO ACHIEVE ABRUPT AND RADICAL ELEVATION...
LURCH!
WITH HERKIMER HOVERING AT HIS ELBOW, THE PROFESSOR PROMPTLY SET THE FRIGIDIA FOR A COURSE THAT DROVE HER AMONG THE THREE PLANETS OF THE FELISIAN GROUP.
GOOD LUCK, APES!
SUDDENLY, AS THE COLD-COPTER CIRCLED ABOVE THE GLOBE OF FELISIA-ALEPH...
LOOK, MENTOR!
WE HAVE FOUND THE TRAIL OF THE ERRANT JEFFERSON!
HUZZAH! WE SHALL YET BE SAVED!
AND AT THAT VERY MOMENT...
SHIP AHOY!
TAKE NO ONE ALIVE! KILL 'EM ALL!
WHILE BACK AGAIN IN BUFFALO FALLS, PA.
YOU MAY CEASE DISMANTLING, WINCHESTER! I HAVE FOUND THE NOTEBOOK!
I WAS STANDING ON IT ALL THE TIME!
TO BE CONTINUED

THE ADVENTURES OF PROFESSOR THINTWHISTLE AND HIS INCREDIBLE AETHER FLYER

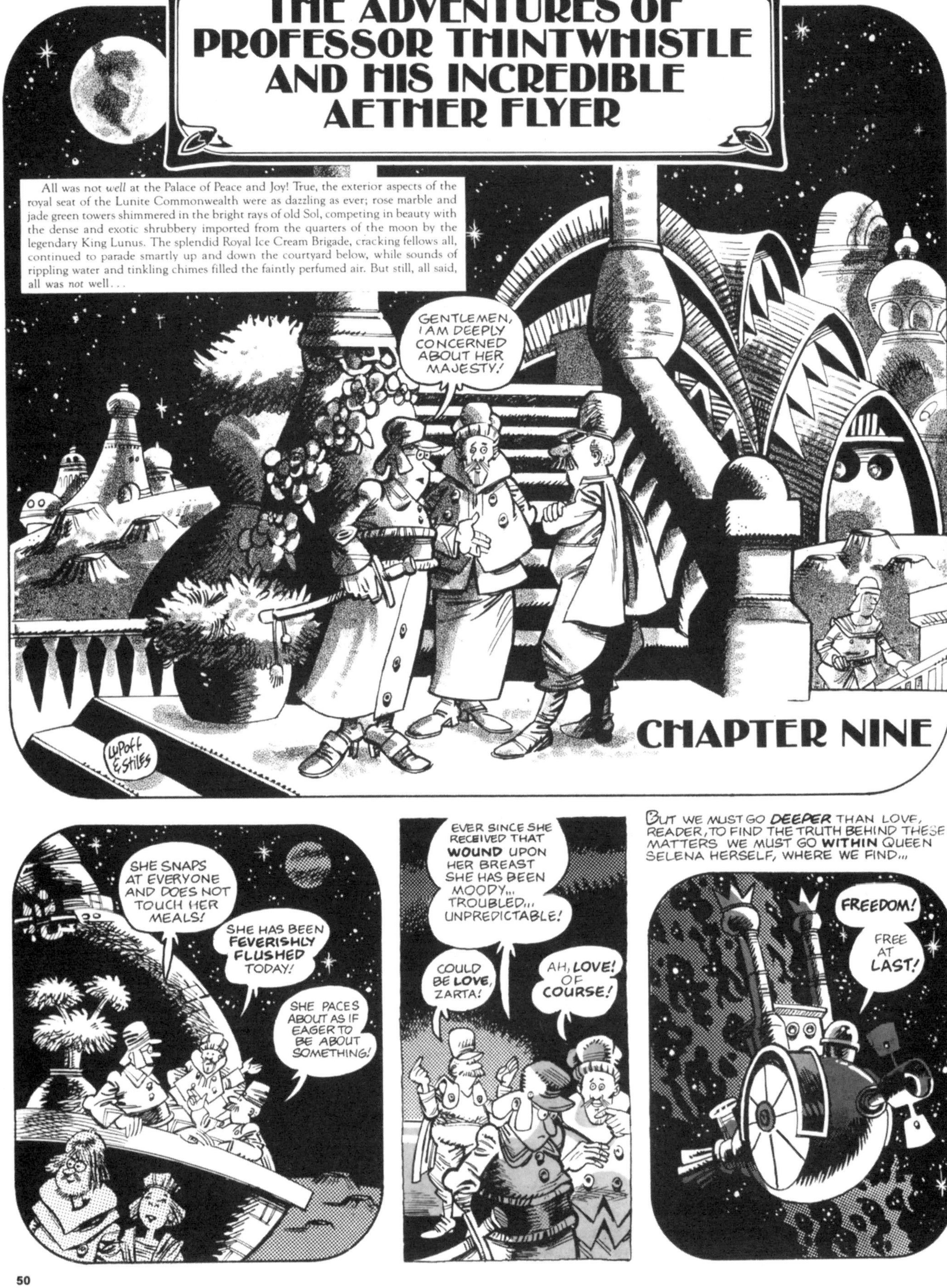

All was not *well* at the Palace of Peace and Joy! True, the exterior aspects of the royal seat of the Lunite Commonwealth were as dazzling as ever; rose marble and jade green towers shimmered in the bright rays of old Sol, competing in beauty with the dense and exotic shrubbery imported from the quarters of the moon by the legendary King Lunus. The splendid Royal Ice Cream Brigade, cracking fellows all, continued to parade smartly up and down the courtyard below, while sounds of rippling water and tinkling chimes filled the faintly perfumed air. But still, all said, all was *not* well . . .
GENTLEMEN, I AM DEEPLY CONCERNED ABOUT HER MAJESTY!
LUPOFF & STILES
CHAPTER NINE
SHE SNAPS AT EVERYONE AND DOES NOT TOUCH HER MEALS!
SHE HAS BEEN **FEVERISHLY FLUSHED** TODAY!
SHE PACES ABOUT AS IF EAGER TO BE ABOUT SOMETHING!
EVER SINCE SHE RECEIVED THAT **WOUND** UPON HER BREAST SHE HAS BEEN MOODY... TROUBLED... UNPREDICTABLE!
COULD BE **LOVE**, ZARTA!
AH, **LOVE!** OF **COURSE!**
BUT WE MUST GO **DEEPER** THAN LOVE, READER, TO FIND THE TRUTH BEHIND THESE MATTERS WE MUST GO **WITHIN** QUEEN SELENA HERSELF, WHERE WE FIND...
FREEDOM!
FREE AT **LAST!**

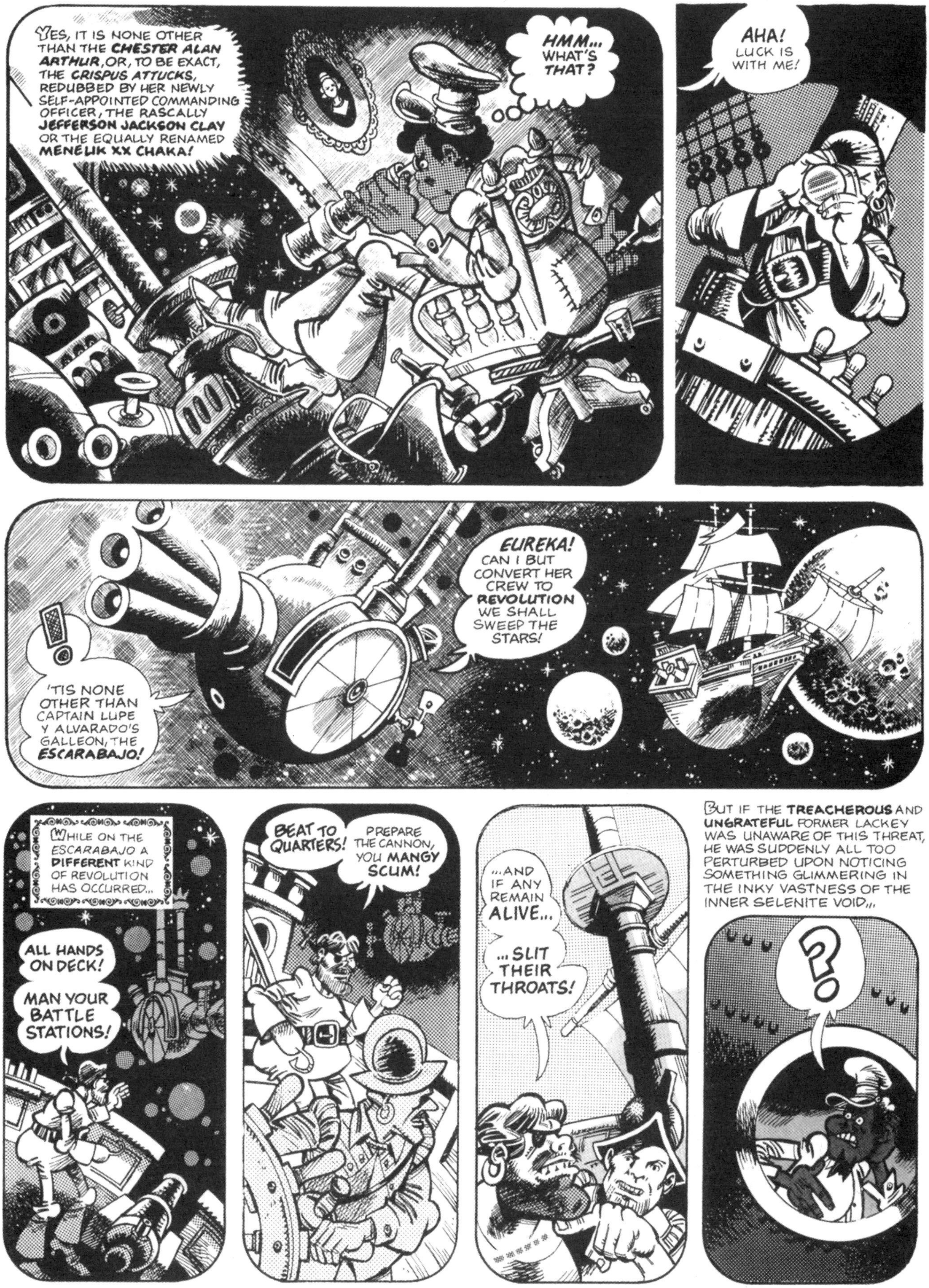

YES, IT IS NONE OTHER THAN THE CHESTER ALAN ARTHUR, OR, TO BE EXACT, THE CRISPUS ATTUCKS, REDUBBED BY HER NEWLY SELF-APPOINTED COMMANDING OFFICER, THE RASCALLY JEFFERSON JACKSON CLAY OR THE EQUALLY RENAMED MENELIK XX CHAKA!
HMM... WHAT'S THAT?
AHA! LUCK IS WITH ME!
EUREKA! CAN I BUT CONVERT HER CREW TO REVOLUTION WE SHALL SWEEP THE STARS!
!
'TIS NONE OTHER THAN CAPTAIN LUPE Y ALVARADO'S GALLEON, THE ESCARABAJO!
WHILE ON THE ESCARABAJO A DIFFERENT KIND OF REVOLUTION HAS OCCURRED...
ALL HANDS ON DECK!
MAN YOUR BATTLE STATIONS!
BEAT TO QUARTERS!
PREPARE THE CANNON, YOU MANGY SCUM!
...AND IF ANY REMAIN ALIVE...
...SLIT THEIR THROATS!
BUT IF THE TREACHEROUS AND UNGRATEFUL FORMER LACKEY WAS UNAWARE OF THIS THREAT, HE WAS SUDDENLY ALL TOO PERTURBED UPON NOTICING SOMETHING GLIMMERING IN THE INKY VASTNESS OF THE INNER SELENITE VOID...
?

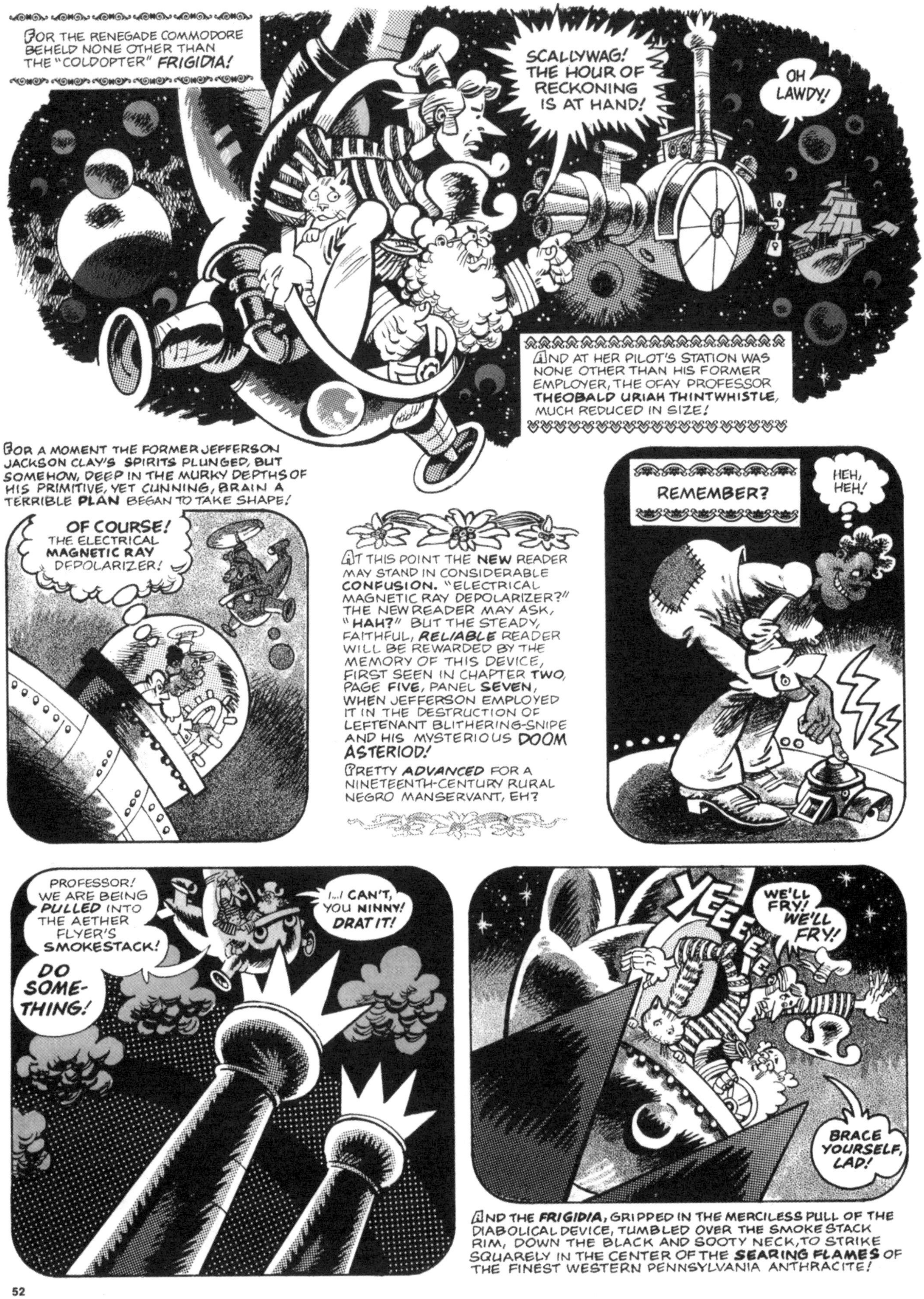

FOR THE RENEGADE COMMODORE BEHELD NONE OTHER THAN THE "COLDOPTER" FRIGIDIA!
SCALLYWAG! THE HOUR OF RECKONING IS AT HAND!
OH LAWDY!
AND AT HER PILOT'S STATION WAS NONE OTHER THAN HIS FORMER EMPLOYER, THE OFAY PROFESSOR THEOBALD URIAH THINTWHISTLE, MUCH REDUCED IN SIZE!
FOR A MOMENT THE FORMER JEFFERSON JACKSON CLAY'S SPIRITS PLUNGED, BUT SOMEHOW, DEEP IN THE MURKY DEPTHS OF HIS PRIMITIVE, YET CUNNING, BRAIN A TERRIBLE PLAN BEGAN TO TAKE SHAPE!
OF COURSE! THE ELECTRICAL MAGNETIC RAY DEPOLARIZER!
AT THIS POINT THE NEW READER MAY STAND IN CONSIDERABLE CONFUSION. "ELECTRICAL MAGNETIC RAY DEPOLARIZER?" THE NEW READER MAY ASK, "HAH?" BUT THE STEADY, FAITHFUL, RELIABLE READER WILL BE REWARDED BY THE MEMORY OF THIS DEVICE, FIRST SEEN IN CHAPTER TWO, PAGE FIVE, PANEL SEVEN, WHEN JEFFERSON EMPLOYED IT IN THE DESTRUCTION OF LEFTENANT BLITHERING-SNIPE AND HIS MYSTERIOUS DOOM ASTERIOD!
PRETTY ADVANCED FOR A NINETEENTH-CENTURY RURAL NEGRO MANSERVANT, EH?
REMEMBER?
HEH, HEH!
PROFESSOR! WE ARE BEING PULLED INTO THE AETHER FLYER'S SMOKESTACK!
DO SOME-THING!
I...I CAN'T, YOU NINNY! DRAT IT!
YEEEEEE
WE'LL FRY! WE'LL FRY!
BRACE YOURSELF, LAD!
AND THE FRIGIDIA, GRIPPED IN THE MERCILESS PULL OF THE DIABOLICAL DEVICE, TUMBLED OVER THE SMOKE STACK RIM, DOWN THE BLACK AND SOOTY NECK, TO STRIKE SQUARELY IN THE CENTER OF THE SEARING FLAMES OF THE FINEST WESTERN PENNSYLVANIA ANTHRACITE!

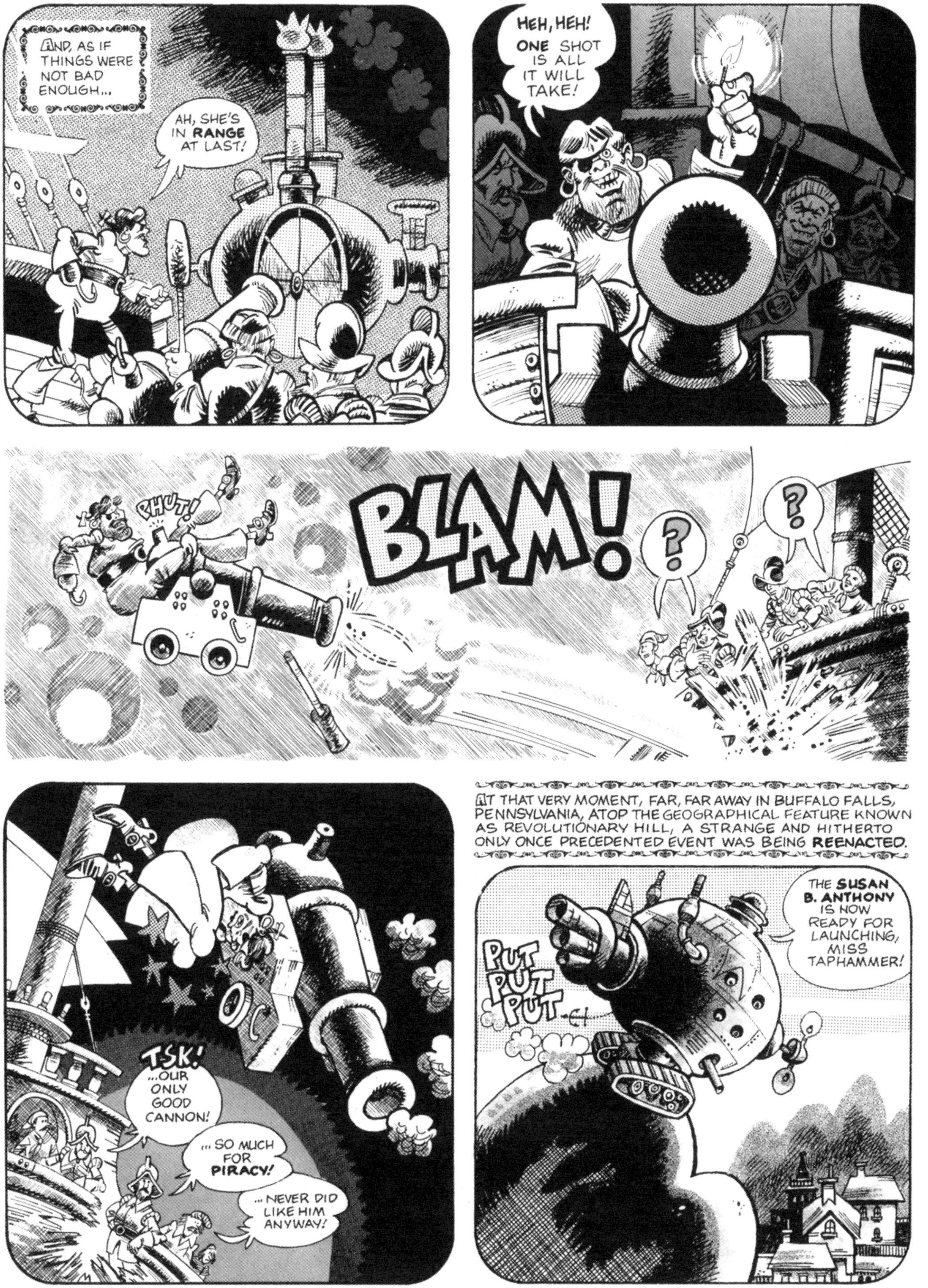
AND, AS IF THINGS WERE NOT BAD ENOUGH...
AH, SHE'S IN **RANGE** AT LAST!
HEH, HEH! **ONE** SHOT IS ALL IT WILL TAKE!
PHUT!
BLAM!
?
?
TSK! ...OUR ONLY GOOD CANNON!
...SO MUCH FOR **PIRACY!**
...NEVER DID LIKE HIM ANYWAY!
AT THAT VERY MOMENT, FAR, FAR AWAY IN BUFFALO FALLS, PENNSYLVANIA, ATOP THE GEOGRAPHICAL FEATURE KNOWN AS REVOLUTIONARY HILL, A STRANGE AND HITHERTO ONLY ONCE PRECEDENTED EVENT WAS BEING **REENACTED.**
PUT PUT PUT
THE **SUSAN B. ANTHONY** IS NOW READY FOR LAUNCHING, MISS TAPHAMMER!

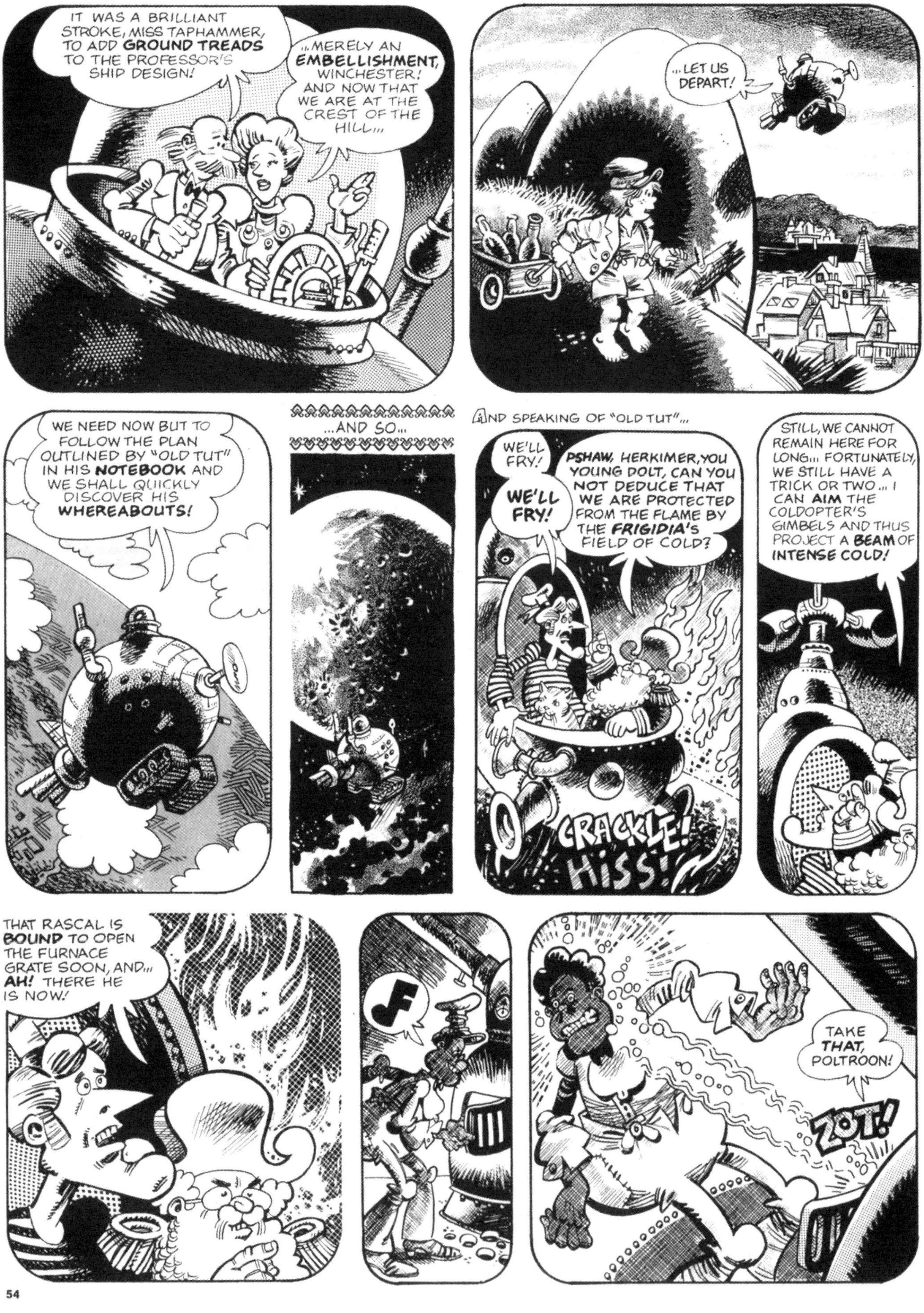

IT WAS A BRILLIANT STROKE, MISS TAPHAMMER, TO ADD GROUND TREADS TO THE PROFESSOR'S SHIP DESIGN!
...MERELY AN EMBELLISHMENT, WINCHESTER! AND NOW THAT WE ARE AT THE CREST OF THE HILL...
...LET US DEPART!
WE NEED NOW BUT TO FOLLOW THE PLAN OUTLINED BY "OLD TUT" IN HIS NOTEBOOK AND WE SHALL QUICKLY DISCOVER HIS WHEREABOUTS!
...AND SO...
AND SPEAKING OF "OLD TUT"...
WE'LL FRY!
WE'LL FRY!
PSHAW, HERKIMER, YOU YOUNG DOLT, CAN YOU NOT DEDUCE THAT WE ARE PROTECTED FROM THE FLAME BY THE FRIGIDIA'S FIELD OF COLD?
CRACKLE! HISS!
STILL, WE CANNOT REMAIN HERE FOR LONG... FORTUNATELY, WE STILL HAVE A TRICK OR TWO... I CAN AIM THE COLDOPTER'S GIMBELS AND THUS PROJECT A BEAM OF INTENSE COLD!
THAT RASCAL IS BOUND TO OPEN THE FURNACE GRATE SOON, AND... AH! THERE HE IS NOW!
TAKE THAT, POLTROON!
ZOT!

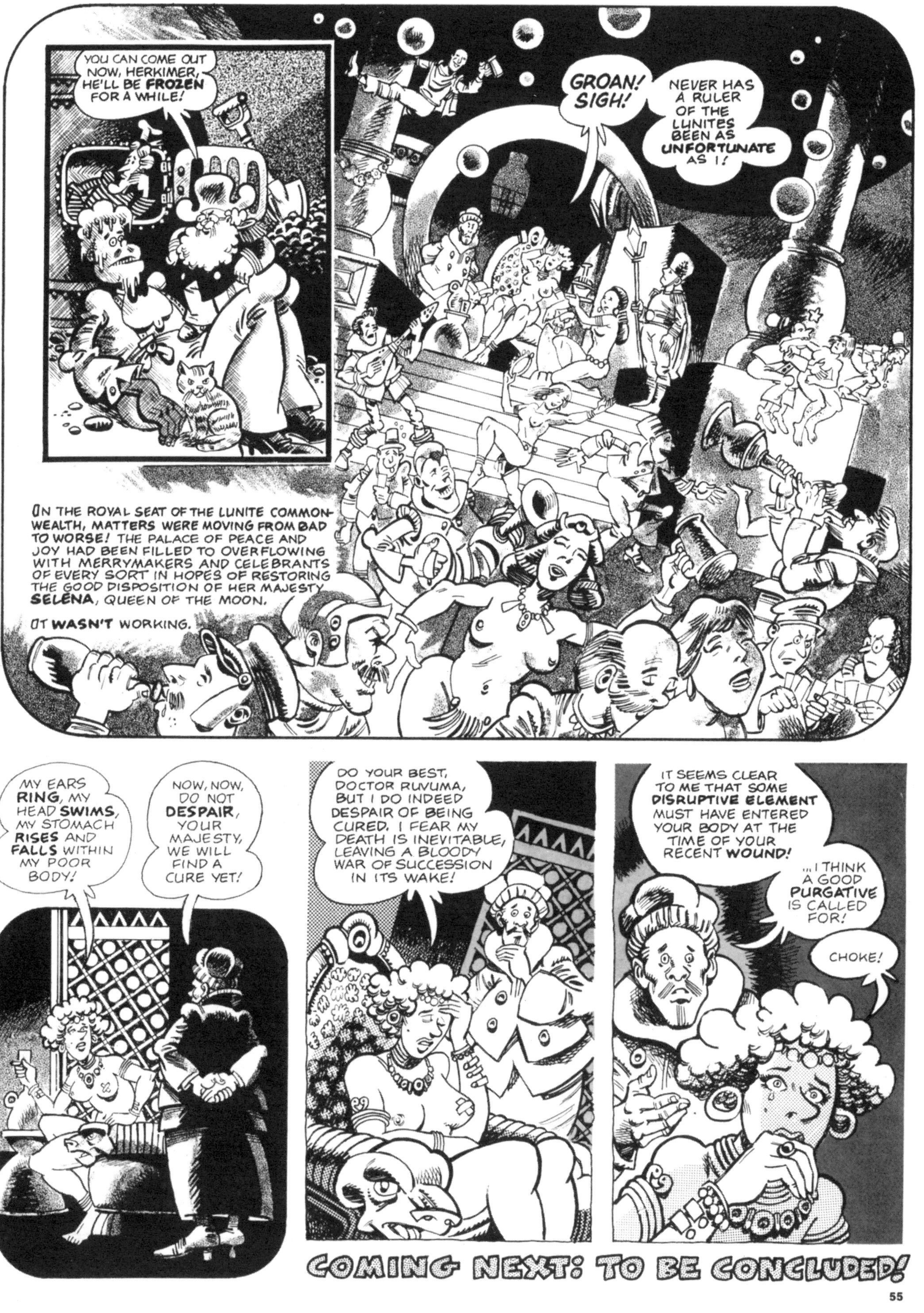
YOU CAN COME OUT NOW, HERKIMER, HE'LL BE FROZEN FOR A WHILE!
GROAN! SIGH!
NEVER HAS A RULER OF THE LUNITES BEEN AS UNFORTUNATE AS I!
ON THE ROYAL SEAT OF THE LUNITE COMMONWEALTH, MATTERS WERE MOVING FROM BAD TO WORSE! THE PALACE OF PEACE AND JOY HAD BEEN FILLED TO OVERFLOWING WITH MERRYMAKERS AND CELEBRANTS OF EVERY SORT IN HOPES OF RESTORING THE GOOD DISPOSITION OF HER MAJESTY SELENA, QUEEN OF THE MOON.
IT WASN'T WORKING.
MY EARS RING, MY HEAD SWIMS, MY STOMACH RISES AND FALLS WITHIN MY POOR BODY!
NOW, NOW, DO NOT DESPAIR, YOUR MAJESTY, WE WILL FIND A CURE YET!
DO YOUR BEST, DOCTOR RUVUMA, BUT I DO INDEED DESPAIR OF BEING CURED. I FEAR MY DEATH IS INEVITABLE, LEAVING A BLOODY WAR OF SUCCESSION IN ITS WAKE!
IT SEEMS CLEAR TO ME THAT SOME DISRUPTIVE ELEMENT MUST HAVE ENTERED YOUR BODY AT THE TIME OF YOUR RECENT WOUND!
...I THINK A GOOD PURGATIVE IS CALLED FOR!
CHOKE!
COMING NEXT: TO BE CONCLUDED!

THE ADVENTURES OF PROFESSOR THINTWHISTLE AND HIS INCREDIBLE AETHER FLYER

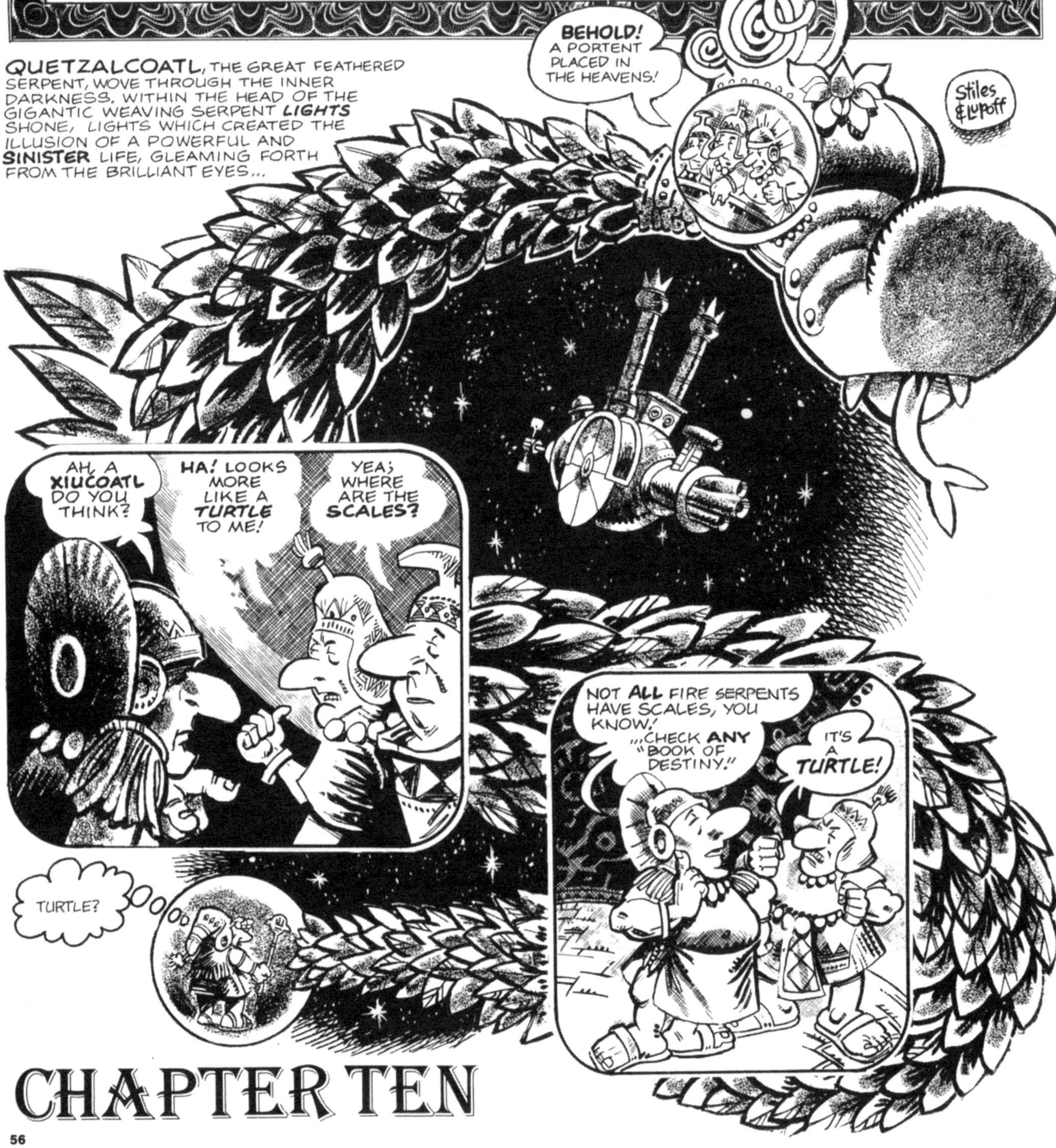
QUETZALCOATL, THE GREAT FEATHERED SERPENT, WOVE THROUGH THE INNER DARKNESS. WITHIN THE HEAD OF THE GIGANTIC WEAVING SERPENT LIGHTS SHONE, LIGHTS WHICH CREATED THE ILLUSION OF A POWERFUL AND SINISTER LIFE, GLEAMING FORTH FROM THE BRILLIANT EYES...
BEHOLD! A PORTENT PLACED IN THE HEAVENS!
Stiles & Lupoff
AH, A XIUCOATL DO YOU THINK?
HA! LOOKS MORE LIKE A TURTLE TO ME!
YEA; WHERE ARE THE SCALES?
NOT ALL FIRE SERPENTS HAVE SCALES, YOU KNOW! ...CHECK ANY "BOOK OF DESTINY!"
IT'S A TURTLE!
TURTLE?

CHAPTER TEN

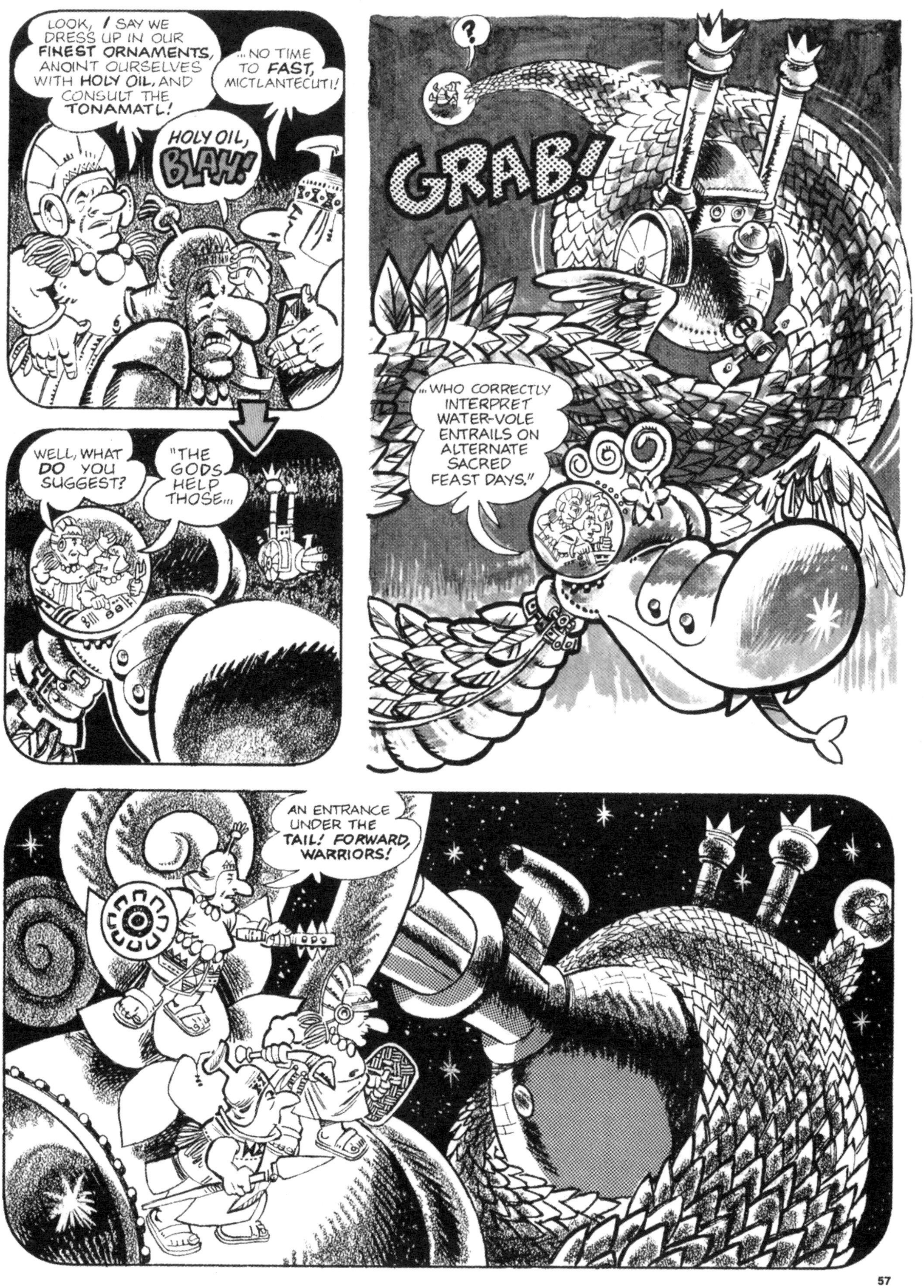
LOOK, I SAY WE DRESS UP IN OUR FINEST ORNAMENTS, ANOINT OURSELVES WITH HOLY OIL, AND CONSULT THE TONAMATL!
...NO TIME TO FAST, MICTLANTECUTI!
HOLY OIL, BLAH!
?
GRAB!
WELL, WHAT DO YOU SUGGEST?
"THE GODS HELP THOSE...
...WHO CORRECTLY INTERPRET WATER-VOLE ENTRAILS ON ALTERNATE SACRED FEAST DAYS."
AN ENTRANCE UNDER THE TAIL! FORWARD, WARRIORS!

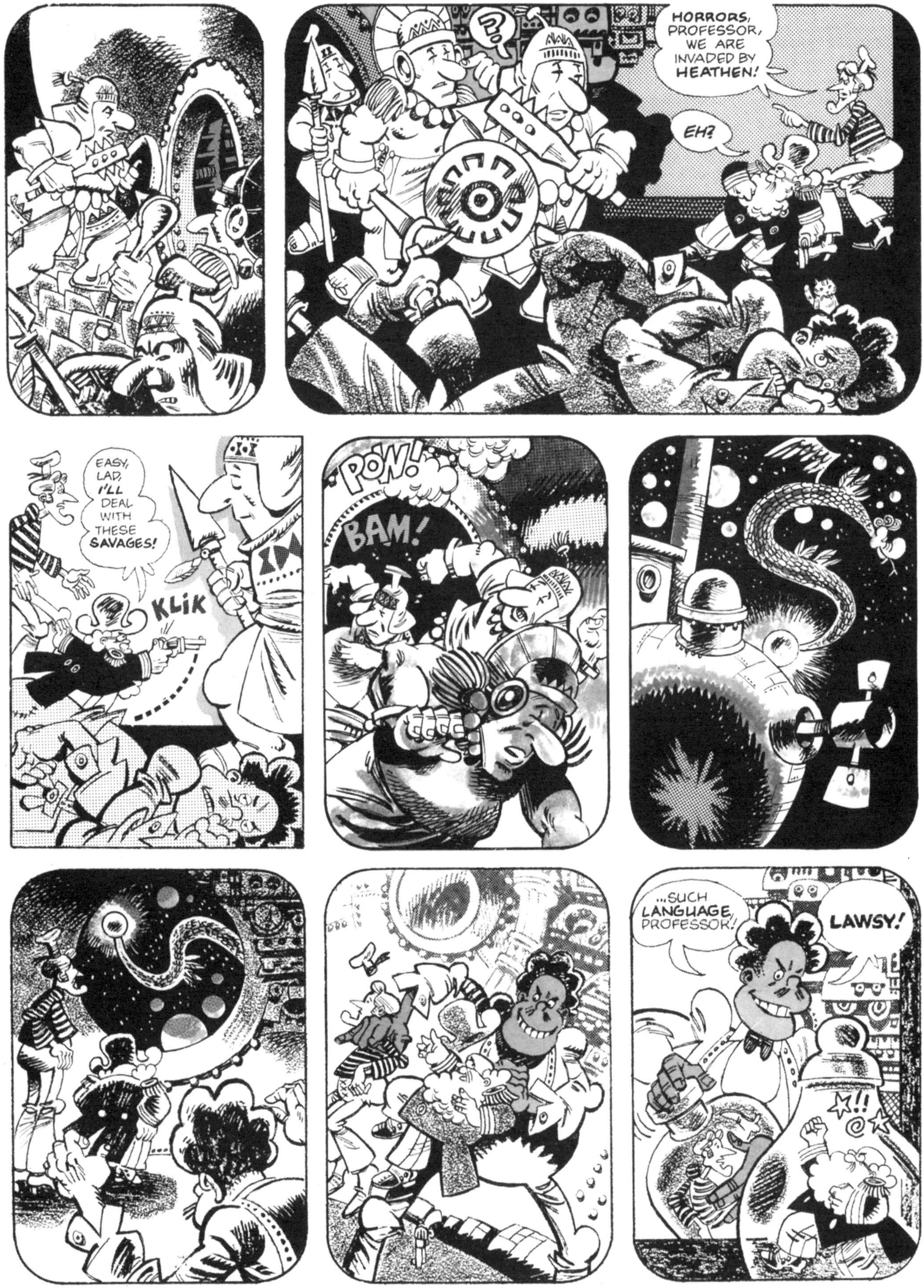

HORRORS, PROFESSOR, WE ARE INVADED BY HEATHEN!
EH?
EASY, LAD, I'LL DEAL WITH THESE SAVAGES!
KLIK
POW!
BAM!
...SUCH LANGUAGE, PROFESSOR!
LAWSY!

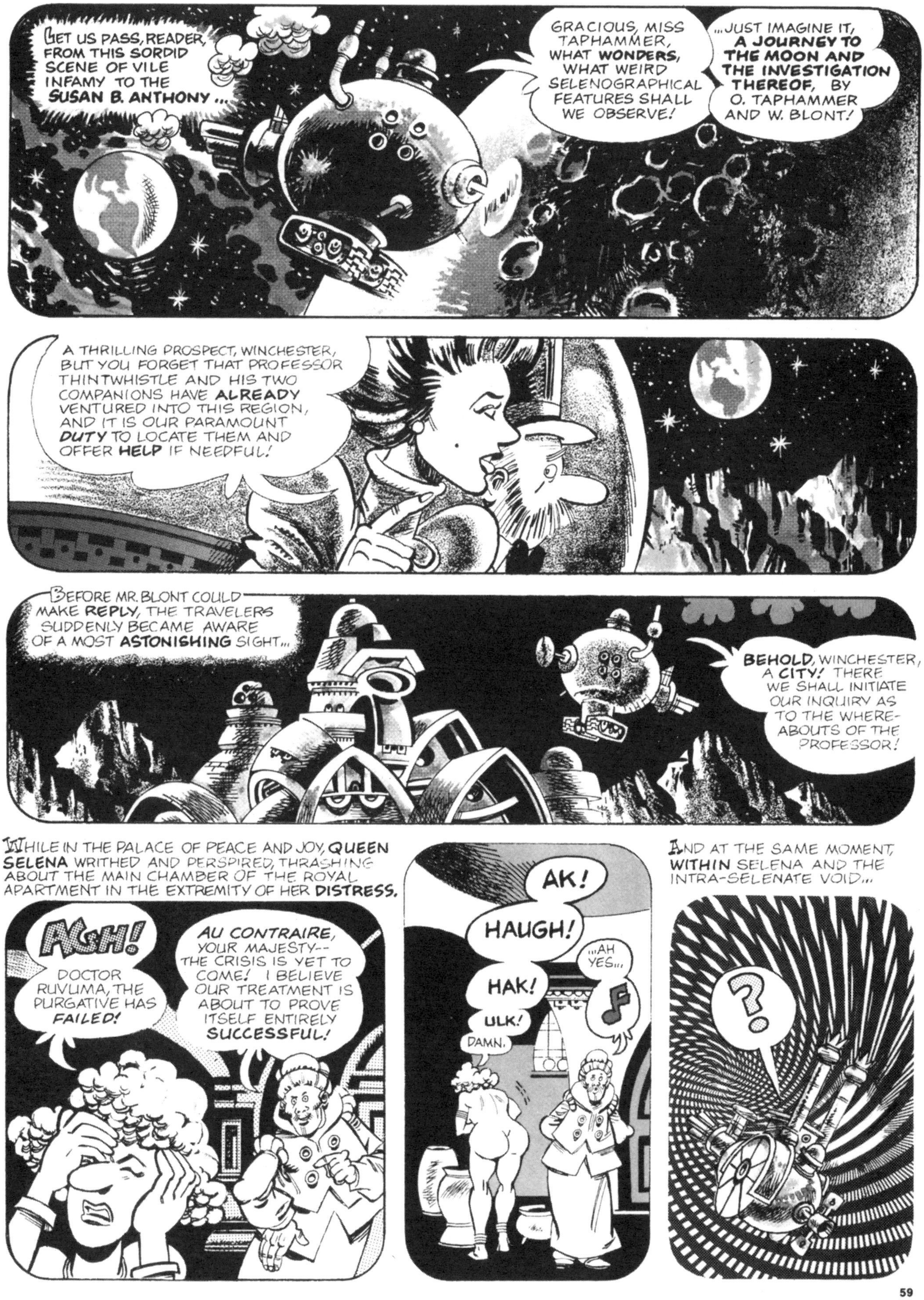

LET US PASS, READER, FROM THIS SORDID SCENE OF VILE INFAMY TO THE SUSAN B. ANTHONY...
GRACIOUS, MISS TAPHAMMER, WHAT WONDERS, WHAT WEIRD SELENOGRAPHICAL FEATURES SHALL WE OBSERVE!
...JUST IMAGINE IT, A JOURNEY TO THE MOON AND THE INVESTIGATION THEREOF, BY O. TAPHAMMER AND W. BLONT!
A THRILLING PROSPECT, WINCHESTER, BUT YOU FORGET THAT PROFESSOR THINTWHISTLE AND HIS TWO COMPANIONS HAVE ALREADY VENTURED INTO THIS REGION, AND IT IS OUR PARAMOUNT DUTY TO LOCATE THEM AND OFFER HELP IF NEEDFUL!
BEFORE MR. BLONT COULD MAKE REPLY, THE TRAVELERS SUDDENLY BECAME AWARE OF A MOST ASTONISHING SIGHT...
BEHOLD, WINCHESTER, A CITY! THERE WE SHALL INITIATE OUR INQUIRY AS TO THE WHEREABOUTS OF THE PROFESSOR!
WHILE IN THE PALACE OF PEACE AND JOY, QUEEN SELENA WRITHED AND PERSPIRED, THRASHING ABOUT THE MAIN CHAMBER OF THE ROYAL APARTMENT IN THE EXTREMITY OF HER DISTRESS.
AGH!
DOCTOR RUVUMA, THE PURGATIVE HAS FAILED!
AU CONTRAIRE, YOUR MAJESTY-- THE CRISIS IS YET TO COME! I BELIEVE OUR TREATMENT IS ABOUT TO PROVE ITSELF ENTIRELY SUCCESSFUL!
AK!
HAUGH!
...AH YES...
HAK!
ULK!
DAMN.
AND AT THE SAME MOMENT, WITHIN SELENA AND THE INTRA-SELENATE VOID...
?

AND WITHIN THE **CHESTER ALAN ARTHUR** JEFFERSON AND HIS TWO PRISONERS WERE HURLED ABOUT AS COSMIC WINDS OF HURRICANE PROPORTION SHOOK THEIR CRAFT, TWISTING THE VERY FABRIC OF THE INTRA-SELENATE VOID!

FINALLY!

ULP!

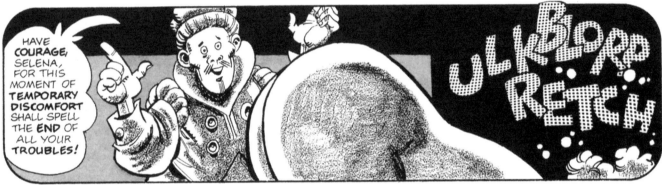

HAVE **COURAGE,** SELENA, FOR THIS MOMENT OF **TEMPORARY DISCOMFORT** SHALL SPELL THE **END** OF ALL YOUR TROUBLES!

ULKBLORP RETCH

?

CLANK!

YOW!

WHY, IT'S A TINY PERSON!

UH., REVOLUTIONARY GREETINGS! IN THE NAME OF TOILERS I OFFER THESE GIFTS!

HELP!

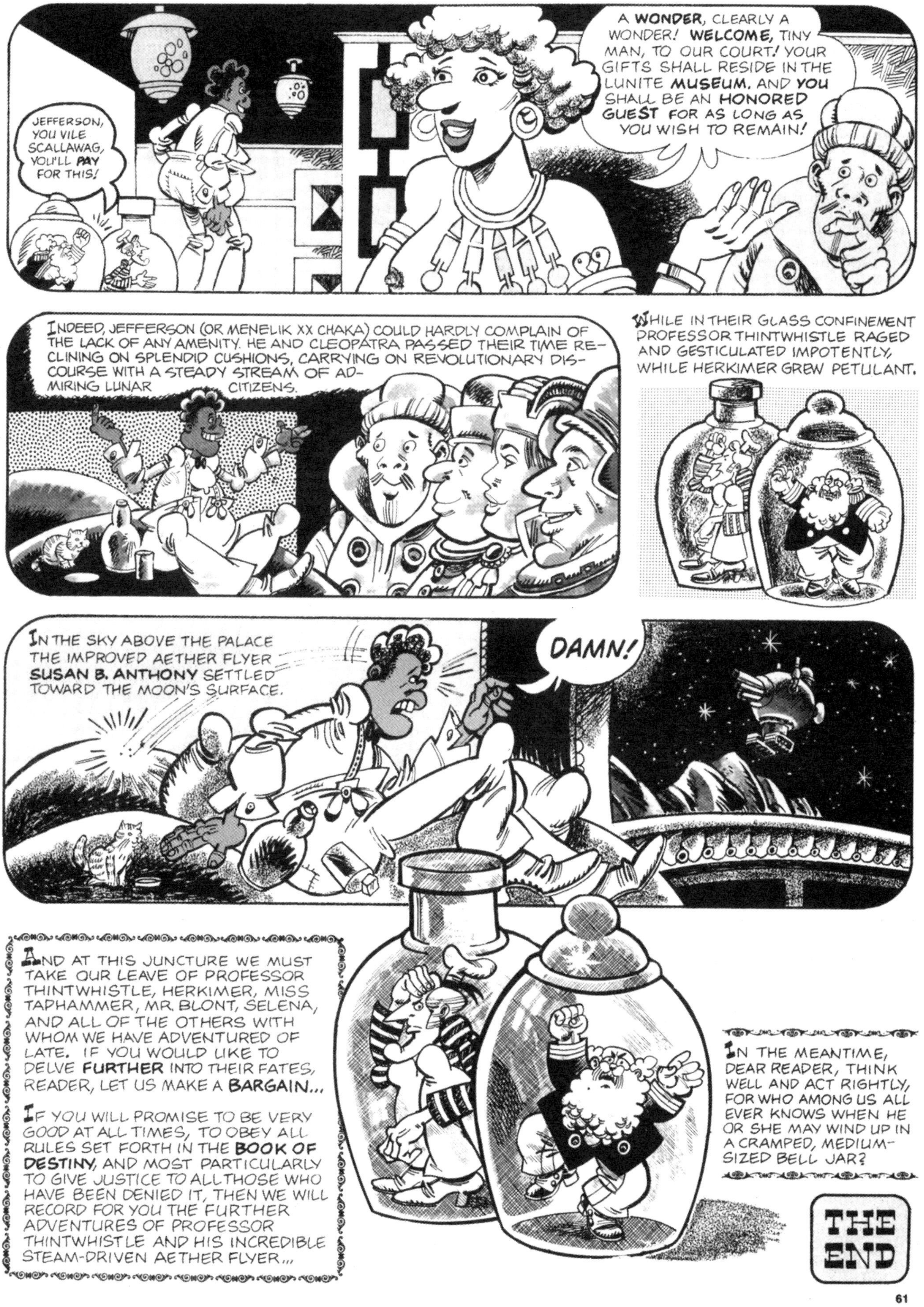

A WONDER, CLEARLY A WONDER! WELCOME, TINY MAN, TO OUR COURT! YOUR GIFTS SHALL RESIDE IN THE LUNITE MUSEUM. AND YOU SHALL BE AN HONORED GUEST FOR AS LONG AS YOU WISH TO REMAIN!
JEFFERSON, YOU VILE SCALLAWAG, YOU'LL PAY FOR THIS!
INDEED, JEFFERSON (OR MENELIK XX CHAKA) COULD HARDLY COMPLAIN OF THE LACK OF ANY AMENITY. HE AND CLEOPATRA PASSED THEIR TIME RECLINING ON SPLENDID CUSHIONS, CARRYING ON REVOLUTIONARY DISCOURSE WITH A STEADY STREAM OF ADMIRING LUNAR CITIZENS.
WHILE IN THEIR GLASS CONFINEMENT PROFESSOR THINTWHISTLE RAGED AND GESTICULATED IMPOTENTLY, WHILE HERKIMER GREW PETULANT.
IN THE SKY ABOVE THE PALACE THE IMPROVED AETHER FLYER SUSAN B. ANTHONY SETTLED TOWARD THE MOON'S SURFACE.
DAMN!
AND AT THIS JUNCTURE WE MUST TAKE OUR LEAVE OF PROFESSOR THINTWHISTLE, HERKIMER, MISS TAPHAMMER, MR. BLONT, SELENA, AND ALL OF THE OTHERS WITH WHOM WE HAVE ADVENTURED OF LATE. IF YOU WOULD LIKE TO DELVE FURTHER INTO THEIR FATES, READER, LET US MAKE A BARGAIN...
IF YOU WILL PROMISE TO BE VERY GOOD AT ALL TIMES, TO OBEY ALL RULES SET FORTH IN THE BOOK OF DESTINY, AND MOST PARTICULARLY TO GIVE JUSTICE TO ALL THOSE WHO HAVE BEEN DENIED IT, THEN WE WILL RECORD FOR YOU THE FURTHER ADVENTURES OF PROFESSOR THINTWHISTLE AND HIS INCREDIBLE STEAM-DRIVEN AETHER FLYER...
IN THE MEANTIME, DEAR READER, THINK WELL AND ACT RIGHTLY, FOR WHO AMONG US ALL EVER KNOWS WHEN HE OR SHE MAY WIND UP IN A CRAMPED, MEDIUM-SIZED BELL JAR?
THE END

SEPTEMBER 1966

World Science Fiction Convention in Cleveland, Ohio. Pat and Dick Lupoff, cartoonist Steve Stiles, and novelist Lee Hoffman sit around table in Chinese restaurant. Dick Lupoff talks about immersing self in bizarre old SF novels published 1880-1920 for research project, describes characters, typical plots, etc. Everybody has a good laugh. Lee Hoffman says this would make an amusing parody. Seed is planted.

WINTER 1966-1967.

Lupoff begins writing "The Incredible Adventures of Professor Thintwhistle and His Amazing Aether Flyer." Inspired by some of Lupoff's old illustrated boy's books, Stiles draws a comic strip version. The first 16 or so pages are published in a mimeographed fan magazine called Horib. Most installments are signed, for reasons that are likely of interest to no one 25 years later, "Fenton Farnworth and Pascal Pascudniak."

1968-1969

After several unfruitful attempts to peddle the yarn either as a syndicated comic strip or a graphic novel, Dell Books offers to buy it as a novel if Lupoff will write it as such. Reluctantly, Lupoff agrees.

JANUARY 1974

After minor delays, the book appears as *Into the Aether*, by Richard A. Lupoff; a slim comics connection is maintained through the choice of cover artist: one Frank Frazetta.

JULY, 1979

Ted White asks Stiles and Lupoff to re-create the comic strip version for *Heavy Metal*, which he is editing at the time. Stiles re-draws the first 16 pages, then adapts another few chapters from the novel and draws them; eventually finds the task of adaptation uncongenial and requests that Lupoff take over, which he does. The story runs as a serial in *Heavy Metal* from February to December, 1980.

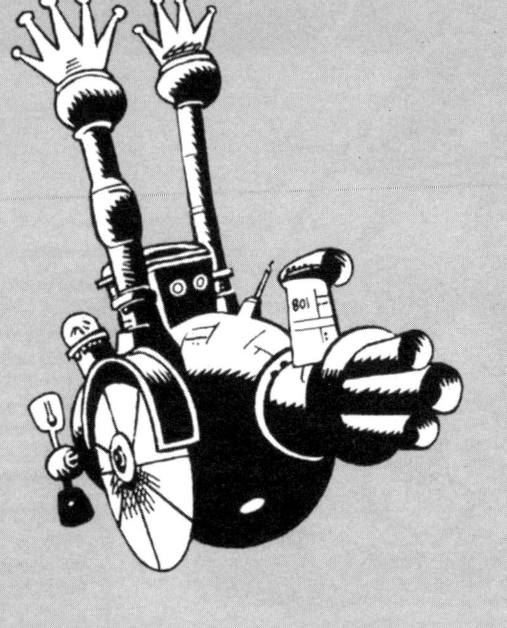
801

MAY, 1985

Verlag Ullstein GmbH edition of the novel version is published in Germany. German title is *Vorstoss in den Ather*, which means something along the lines of "knocked into the aether."

1990

When Steve Stiles submits a new drawing of Thintwhistle & Co. to Fantagraphics editor Kim Thompson for an unrelated project, Thompson, a *Thintwhistle* fan since its *Heavy Metal* appearance, asks Lupoff and Stiles if they would like it to be released as a graphic album. They would.

SEPTEMBER 1991

Precisely one quarter-century after that Cleveland conversation, *Thintwhistle* is released in the form for which it was initially conceived: as a 64-page graphic album.